Witchful Thinking

A Witches of Whisper Grove Novel

ANDRIS BEAR

Witchful Thinking

Prologue

Evangeline crept her car to a stop at the curb, then put it in park. Leaving the wipers on high to combat the pounding rain, she peered at the house with a mix of awe and dread.

Winther house.

Her house.

Actually, hers and her sisters'. The lawyer of their parent's estate had made that very clear. Upon their parents' death, the house became the property of his daughters—not one but all four, together. Evangeline was fine with shared ownership. The thought of living in this monstrous house by herself was not only spooky, but also lonely. However, even with her sisters in

1

residence—assuming they all decided to stay with her in Whisper Grove—Evangeline wasn't sure she wanted to live in the house.

Not after everything they'd lost to get it.

Paul and Lily Winther died in what authorities had officially dubbed an electrical fire. Unofficially, they could give no reason for the blaze that burned Evangeline's childhood home to the ground and stolen her parents. No traces of accelerant had been found, nor could the fire investigator find the point of origin.

It was as if the flames had burst into existence with the sole purpose of consuming everything Evangeline held dear.

The only saving grace was that Alex had been at work and the twins at school. If she had lost them, too...

Evangeline shook her head, trying to dispel the morbid thoughts. The last thing she needed was to look for heartbreak where there was none. Rather, she willed her pulse to calm, focusing instead on the remainder of her family and how lucky she was to have them.

What she couldn't quiet was her mind. It threw out questions on a continuous loop, torturing her with *whats, whys, and ifs.* What had caused the fire? Why had her parents been home? If they had gone into work, where they should have been midmorning on a Tuesday...

"Is that it?" Alex asked from the passenger seat.

Dragging her gaze to her sister, Evangeline nodded. Alex was focused on the house, so Evangeline added, "Yes."

Alex leaned forward, squinting through the rain-splashed windshield. "It's enormous."

"It's *gorgeous*," Elle piped in from the backseat. "You've been inside?"

Smiling, Evangeline met her youngest sister's wide eyes in the rearview mirror. "Yes. It's very—"

"How did you get in?" Alex demanded, resettling in her seat. Her hazel eyes narrowed shrewdly.

Irked at the scrutiny, Evangeline straightened and announced, "It was unlocked."

The gate *and* door had unlocked, so if she were being technical—*she was*—it wasn't a lie.

It just wasn't the truth, either. Not entirely.

Alex didn't need details. If Evangeline's previous visit was any indication, Alex, Elle, and Mal would figure out the house had its own personality soon enough.

"Come on," she said, pulling her keys from the ignition and shoving them into her pocket before climbing from the car. "Make it snappy. I don't want to get soaked."

Her body swayed a little as she waited for her sisters to

do the same, and she wondered if the coffee she'd had before meeting with the lawyer was going to stay in her stomach. Probably should have eaten something but at the time, the thought of food had put her off.

"Afraid you'll melt?" Mal asked, shutting her door and coming around stand with her.

Evangeline stared at her. If Mal had any idea how apt that reference was…

"No," she said, grabbing Mal's hand and tugging her toward the gate entrance. "I'm afraid you will."

Mal snorted, and Evangeline smiled at her typical response. Mal was the calm storm of the bunch. Like a layer of ice under the snow, she was hard to crack, but once she did—*run.* Because nothing short of God stepping in would stop her.

While she respected Mal's frugal doling out of comeuppance, Evangeline liked to think of herself as having a little more self-control. Sure, she had emotions like everyone else, but they didn't rule her.

It seemed she was the only one who valued her head-over-heart mantra as Alex boasted a hair trigger and a temper that could rival the Hulk's. Though Alex referred to her outbursts as bouts of passion, they all knew she liked to argue. If that involved throwing a punch or two or yanking out a chunk of hair, so be it.

4

The only one who avoided confrontation was Ellery. Sweet Elle wore her heart on her sleeve and her brain, often, in another outfit. The girl was the epitome of naïve and tender, which was why God had given her three sisters who would pulverize anyone who tried to take advantage of her.

Now, they were all each other had.

Evangeline felt as though her security had been ripped out from under, leaving her dangling in the air over an uncertain cliff. Though they hadn't spoken of it, she knew her sisters felt the same.

Blowing out a shaky breath, Evangeline peered at each in turn. She wished for something encouraging to say, something that would give them hope and a positive outlook for the future.

Instead, she said, "Follow me," and then pushed open the gate, walked up the sidewalk, and headed for the porch. As soon as her foot reached the first step, a soft click sounded above her.

Evangeline jerked her gaze up just as the door crept open. Her heartbeat thrummed in her head, and she glanced behind to see if any of her sisters noticed.

They were busy trying to take in every detail of the house. Even Mallory couldn't keep her eyes from sliding from one end to the other.

5

Pushing through the doorway, Evangeline entered the roomy foyer. A rush of warmth settled over her, forcing the chill of the rainy day aside. A heartfelt sigh left her lips. The tension in her muscles slowly uncoiled.

Until she spotted *him.*

"Chester," she growled, stomping over to the cat. "Where have you been?"

From the moment she'd returned to her apartment with her sisters in tow, she hadn't been able to find the damn cat. She'd torn the place apart, worried that something had happened to him.

Jerkhole.

Chester stretched his spine with a yawned cat noise. It might have been a demand for food or the promise to poop on her pillow.

"Is this the kitty you told us about?" Elle dropped to her knees, scooped the miserable wretch into her arms, and showered him with adoration as she scratched him from one end to the other. "Where did you go, pretty kitty?" she asked.

"Yeah, that's the fleabag." Evangeline didn't know which was worse—her sister's delighted coos or Chester's over-the-top purring. The cat from hell deserved neither. "It's all catnip and cuddles until he starts talking to you."

6

Evangeline ignored them in favor of the item Chester had been sitting next to. The chest was small, maybe two feet by three feet, and made of shiny reddish-brown wood—cherry, maybe, or mahogany. The same spiral symbol she'd seen by the door was carved into the hinged lid that was secured with a tarnished gold lock.

Sticking out from under the corner of the chest was a manila envelope.

Evangeline's hand reached out on its own accord and grabbed the envelope. She watched her fingers peel back the seal, slip into the opening, and then pull out a folded sheet of paper and another smaller envelope.

The paper rattled in her hand. Or more accurately, her hand shook, rattling the paper.

"What is that?" Alex asked, suddenly peering over her shoulder.

Evangeline sidestepped to avoid her sister's prying gaze. She wanted to read it first. "Give me a minute and I'll tell you." Her words came out harsher than intended, but she couldn't worry over that now. Her nerves were raw, and her body was vibrating hard enough to chatter her teeth.

She scanned the typed letter. "It's from Mr. Shaw, Dad's attorney."

Elle released Chester to come stand next to Alex. Mal stayed put, propping her elbow on the fireplace mantel to regard Evangeline with mild curiosity. Well, then. Now that she had their attention, Evangeline read the letter aloud.

"Dear Ms. Winther,

Per your father's request, the last of your inheritance was placed inside the house at 112 Main Street. He did not leave a key with me, so I assume you have it. His only instruction was that the chest not be opened until all four of his daughters were in attendance." With a shrug, she added, "That's it."

"So, let's open it," Alex said, moving forward before Evangeline could beat her to it.

"Do you have a key?" Mal asked.

Evangeline's shouted "No!" stopped everyone in their tracks. Her cheeks flamed. She couldn't say why she wanted, *needed*, to be the one to open the chest, but she did, and if she'd learned nothing else over the last few weeks, it was to trust her gut.

There was something in that chest that was meant for *her*. Not her sisters—just her.

Of course, she didn't give voice to the certainty. She held up the second envelope with *Evangeline* scrawled across the front in her dad's scribbly handwriting.

"There's another letter. It's from Dad."

A weighted hush fell over them as she opened the envelope and freed the folded paper.

Our dearest girls,

First, your mother and I love you very much. Our greatest desire has been only to protect you. I hope you can remember that as time wears on.

If you're reading this, your mother and I are gone. Soon, you will face many things you do not understand. Changes may come on tidal waves or a trickle, but they are coming. You will each develop your own gifts. They will make you a target. But you are strong, so much more so than you realize. You have each other, and there is no force or magic on this earth stronger than family.

In this chest, you will find a journal, a mirror, a ring, and a key. They are conduits and anchors to where you come from.

The journal is mine. Read it carefully. It will help you figure out what you're up against. I should have warned you before now, but I was afraid any mention of the craft would bring it to our doorstep.

With the mirror, anything you see can be brought to life.

The key will reveal the lock.

One ring to rule them all. Just kidding. The ring is a collector. Use it wisely. Not everything taken can be returned.

There are others like us. Find the light. It will burn away the darkness.

Love you all,

Dad

P.S. If you run into Chester, he can be bought with tuna steaks and a stuffed bunny. Don't ask.

Chapter One

Evangeline peered at her reflection, scrutinizing the woman in the mirror. She saw the same curly hair, same brown eyes. She still looked like a naïve college graduate with the world at her fingertips.

But that was all that remained of the woman she'd been four months ago.

Evangeline chuffed at her own melodrama. And she fancied herself the rational one? Maybe she'd lost that as well, because life had gone from order to chaos in a few short weeks, and she wasn't entirely sure anything logical had made the trip.

A glance at the clock beside the bed confirmed she'd been staring off into space for too long. She had ten minutes to finish getting ready, eat something, and chug down some coffee before she had to leave for work.

Her boss at the library, Melissa Handscomb, aka Mimi the Militant, would gleefully fire her if she showed up late one more time. Might even have her pink slip filled out and waiting.

What Mimi failed to realize was Evangeline despised being late as much as Mimi hated her to be. Punctuality was Evangeline's middle name. Except when she was late.

Running a brush through her hair tamed the mess about as well as licking the wall would have—the curls sprang back into place as soon as the bristles passed through them. For the millionth time in her life, she wondered why she'd gotten stuck with the rebellious coif.

All of her sisters had smooth, shiny tresses while hers resembled an electrified steel-wool pad.

She spun from her reflection to grab her shoes from the closet, nearly jumping out of her skin at the figure standing in her doorway.

"Alex," she hissed. "What did I tell you about sneaking up on me?"

Her sister raised a lazy brow. "I was hardly sneaking," she said, canting against the doorframe. "You're as jumpy as a cat."

Evangeline snatched up her black flats before brushing past Alex. "I don't like that word."

"What, jumpy?"

"Cat," she stated, slipping her foot into a shoe.

Alex laughed, pushing off the doorframe to take a seat on her bed. "What did poor Chester ever do to you?"

Peeking over her shoulder, Evangeline eyed her sister. What would Alex say if she answered honestly? That the cat seemed to disappear from one house and appear in another across town. He talked—granted, it was mostly in her head, so she couldn't be sure if she could pin that one on him—and licked himself incessantly. Either the cat had the most meticulous grooming habits of any man, or the furry freak had a fetish. Her brain convulsed at the thought.

Those off-putting attributes aside, he was also psychic. *Ish*. Or whatever the hell he was.

Chester seemed to know exactly when she needed a push. He'd somehow known Evangeline needed to answer the phone that night. Had he realized her parents were dead? If so, how? More so, why hadn't he warned her, so she could have done something to stop the fire?

Of course, not a word of that craziness left her mouth. Instead, she dropped her focus to the bed.

"He licks his ass where you're sitting."

Alex's gaze settled on the navy comforter. She shrugged. "He licks his ass everywhere."

Sadly, she was right. The mangy sod did have a thing for licking.

"Are you done with this?" Her sister started to reach for the journal Evangeline had tossed on the bed. Panic snapped in her nerves and she lunged, scarcely beating Alex to it. That Evangeline looked like a lunatic clutching it to her chest didn't matter—only that it was in her possession, not Alex's.

Alex settled back into her seat, regarding her for long moments. "What is with you and Dad's journal? Why won't you let anyone else see it?"

Because it's full of things you wouldn't believe, even if I swore a blood oath.

Evangeline swallowed. "I'm not finished with it."

"Really?" Alex unfolded her long frame and stood. "You've done nothing but shove your nose in it since we got here. Knowing your voracious reading habits, I bet you've read it five times already."

Seven. But who was counting?

Evangeline hugged it tighter to her chest. "I'll share it, but I need... to understand some things first."

Evangeline pretended not to notice Alex's skeptical expression. What did she care if Alex believed her reason for keeping it close? As long as her sister kept her hands off the journal.

It wasn't that Evangeline didn't want her sisters to know what their dad had written. She just didn't want them to know that it applied to her. Or worse, *only* to her.

Evangeline wanted to assume each of her sisters would inherit abilities as well, but what if she was the only one? How would they react? She would be an outcast in the only family she had left. Would knowing their father had also been a caster save her in their opinion?

Besides, how in the hell *did* one announce they were a witch?

Hey, guess what, that Sabrina chick ain't got nothing on me. I'm a human lie detector. Oh wait—not human 'cause I'm a witch. Ta-da!

Not a conversation she was ready to have. At least, not until she found a way to control it.

"I have to go to work," Evangeline stated, wishing Alex would leave her room so she could hide the journal. Then again, she couldn't think of a single place to hide it that Alex wouldn't find should she decide to snoop. Taking it with her was the only way to keep it from her sister, but the idea of removing it from the house gave her a case of the vapors.

"Whatever." Alex exaggerated her sulk as she turned away.

"Evie, you have a visitor!" drifted up the stairs.

Alex froze, then spun on her with a breathy, "A visitor," and darted from the room.

Evangeline shoved her dad's journal under the mattress, readjusted the wrinkled comforter, then ran after Alex. The hiding spot wouldn't do long term, but it was good enough until she left for work. Unless the little sneak came snooping before then...

Rounding the curve in the staircase, Evangeline almost plowed into said sneak as she'd stopped halfway down, staring at something Evangeline couldn't see.

"What are you doing?" Evangeline demanded, trying to peer over her shoulder. True to form, Alex sashayed left and right, blocking her view. Evangeline considered grabbing her ankles and tipping her over the banister.

"Holy hot balls, who is that?" Alex asked around snickers.

"Let me see, and I'll tell you."

Alex moved down a step. Evangeline crouched to peek into the foyer, and her heart skipped a beat. Okay, it skipped three or four at seeing Shane standing at the front door, his hands tucked into the pockets of a well-worn pair of jeans. His dark hair was still slightly damp from a shower, and he was sporting a five o'clock shadow.

His gaze slipped over Alex before locking in on Evangeline. His lips curved into that sexy smile she'd missed, and she couldn't have stopped her dopey grin if her life had depended on it.

This time, when the urge to shove Alex aside hit her, she ran with it. "He's my mechanic. Get out of the way."

Alex must have sensed her intentions because she squished against the wall to keep from getting trampled, calling Evangeline a few ripe names as she passed. Was it wrong to delight in her sister's muttered curses? She didn't think so.

She ignored Alex, speeding right past a curious Elle. Evangeline's focus was on the man at the door. Her rib cage felt too tight, and her head felt too big. She couldn't catch a full breath.

How had she gone three weeks without seeing him? Since that horrible night Alex had called to tell her about their parents' death, Evangeline's attention had been gobbled up by planning funeral services, dealing with insurance and lawyers, taking possession of the house, moving her sisters to Whisper Grove, and enrolling the younger two in the local high school. The

17

list went on and on to the point she'd had nothing left for the man she adored other than daily texts and a few short phone calls.

Yet, he was here, waiting to see her.

She was breathless by the time she reached him. "Hi."

"Hi. Fancy meeting you here," he said, entirely too handsome to be so unsmooth.

"She lives here," Ellery offered, oblivious that Shane was well aware of that fact. Bless her heart.

Evangeline repressed the urge to roll her eyes. Turning to face her sister, she introduced them. "Shane, this is my sister, Ellery. Elle, this is my Shane."

Shane took Elle's hand. "Nice to meet you. Evie has told me a lot about you."

"Oh, that's good, because I don't think she's mentioned you," Elle said with a perplexed frown.

And now Evangeline wanted to slink across the floor and hide in the closet. But not until she clubbed ditzy Elle over the head with her shoe. "It's not what it sounds like," she assured him. "Everything goes in one ear and out the other with this one."

Not to throw poor Elle under the bus, but... *shove*.

Evangeline didn't think her words smoothed things over

because Shane looked like he'd just gotten a physical exam from a porcupine. A *very* thorough exam.

Sadly, as true as her words were, so were Elle's. She hadn't mentioned Shane much. Not because he wasn't important, but because he was hers—the one person she had all to herself.

Now that she and her sisters were living under the same roof again, God help them, everything was community property. They had to share food, space, *air*. Even though Evangeline had lived on her own for less than six months, the reversion to a houseful of chittering females was overwhelming.

Shane was the one thing she didn't have to share if she didn't want to.

"Actually, Shane," sounded behind her an instant before Alex appeared at her side. "I have heard her mention you. I'm Alex."

Alex thrust her hand at him. Being the gentleman he was, Shane took it. "Nice to meet you, too, Alex."

Even though she could see it coming, Evangeline sucked her teeth when Alex folded his hand in both of hers. Houdini couldn't have escaped that hold, much less a poor, unsuspecting Shane.

"My, you have such strong hands," Alex purred, pulling him in close.

Shane's eyes widened with the realization that Alex was flirting with him. In front of Evangeline. He turned a confused, pleading expression on her, and Evangeline just nodded that yes, he was reading the situation correctly.

A vision of taking a chainsaw to her sister's hair flitted through her mind. Evangeline sighed. That could get so messy. Besides, Alex fought like a hellcat in a 'roid rage. No way Evangeline could take her. So she elbowed Alex in the ribs, "accidentally" smashed her heel onto the harlot's bare foot, and bulldozed her way between them.

Goodness, but Alex yowled loud enough to do Chester proud. "You clumsy moose," she bit out through clenched teeth, limping away.

Winking at Shane, Evangeline said, "And now you know the dynamics of my family. Given another minute of her manhandling, and I'd have shaved her head. Scared yet?"

"As long as you leave *my* hair alone."

Laughter brushed aside her irritation. This man never failed to lift her spirits. When he opened his arms, she went into them without hesitation. He closed them, snuggling her tight against his body. This, this man, and what was between them was what she needed most. It felt right to be his. Why had she held him at bay for so long?

Because fear made people do stupid things.

"I missed you," she admitted. The scent of his soap filled her nostrils. She snuggled deeper, enjoying the warmth of his body seeping into hers.

He kissed the top of her head. "I missed you, too. Can I take you to breakfast?"

"Yes," was on the tip of her tongue, but she was scheduled to open the library today. Regretfully, she drew out of his arms. "I can't. It's my first day back to work. If I'm late, Mimi will have a stroke."

"It's probably for the best. I have a muffler repair scheduled this morning, anyway." Shane stuck out his elbow in invitation. "But I have enough time to drive my girl to work, if she'd like that."

"She would like that." She pointed at the stairs. "Let me get my things, and I'll meet you at the truck?"

She watched him until he was settled in the cab of his truck before spinning on her heel and marching into the kitchen with the full intention to cut a witch. Her ire must have been preceded her, because Elle, who was seated at the table for breakfast, paused with her toast halfway to her mouth.

Evangeline skimmed over her to lock on Alex. "Hussy," she growled.

Alex—the hussy—continued to pour coffee into her

mug as if Evangeline hadn't spoken, as if she didn't fear for her life. Evangeline clenched her fists at her sister's nonchalance, even though she knew her annoyance was the very reaction Alex wanted.

Alex returned the pot to the maker, then let her gaze travel over Evangeline. "Relax, Evie. I have no interest in your mechanic. I only wanted to get a rise out of you." Lifting the mug to her mouth, she blew into the steamy liquid. "He does have great hands, though."

It wasn't that Evangeline thought Alex wanted Shane— it was that Alex had this innate, undeniable impulse to ensure every man she came across noticed her, thought her the most beautiful woman in the world.

The schtick had been old *before* puberty hit Alex, when she was a gangly, angsty teenager, desperate to blossom into a beautiful goddess.

Evangeline made a sound of disgust. "Grow up, Alex. You're too old to be so needy. We're the adults in the house now. Act like it." She might have taken more pleasure in the barb if Alex hadn't appeared so stricken by her words. Snatching her purse off the chair, Evangeline exited the kitchen, tossing, "Why don't you find a job today?" behind her.

"I've been looking," Alex shouted.

"Look harder." Evangeline let the door slam to punctuate her statement as she left the house.

Shane cranked the heat, then rubbed his hands together. In the short time he'd been inside, the cab of his truck had gone from toasty to chilly. He stared at the big house as he waited for Evie.

He'd been staring at that house for as long as he could remember. Even as a kid, he wondered about the place. Why didn't anyone live there? Who owned it?

Of course, there had always been rumors—it was haunted, the owner fled in the middle of the night, Satan lived there with his harem of witches.

The last one gave him a good chuckle. He couldn't state an opinion on the devil, but he'd gotten a crash course on witchcraft lately.

Since he'd accepted he was a guardian—though he still didn't entirely grasp what all that entailed—the world was different. More vivid, more active, and definitely more... *weird*. Colors were both brighter and darker, sounds resonated more, but so did silence. And when he touched certain objects, he felt its vibration in his bones.

He honestly didn't know if something in him had awakened the world around him, or if the world had forced him to open his eyes and pay attention, but his senses were in a constant state of awareness that was both exhilarating and exhausting.

His uncle, also a guardian and protector of casters at one time, had warned Shane it could be a rough transition. He hadn't realized how rough until even his sleep was plagued with worry over protecting Evangeline.

His witch.

At least, he hoped. Her reaction to him showing up unannounced was a good sign. They had just started to get serious when her parents died. He'd tried to be supportive and give her space, but a part of him had feared the distance would eventually grow. Unfortunately, even after she'd returned to Whisper Grove with her sisters, that fear continued to fester. Because she had been so distant.

She would text, even take his calls, but her heart wasn't in the conversations. At least, not like it had been before. Yeah, it was selfish of him to worry over their relationship when she clearly had so much more to deal with, but he was starting to get a complex.

In his defense, he hadn't stopped in *just* to gauge her reaction to him. He'd needed to see with his own eyes that she was all right. Though she was as new to this darker world of witchcraft as he was, the burden she carried was much heavier.

Especially now that her sisters were her sole responsibility.

Evangeline popped out onto the porch, pulling the door shut behind her. The wind caught her hair, whirling it into a curly tornado, and he chuckled as she tried to tame it one-handed. "Never gonna happen, baby," he muttered.

If she had any clue how glorious she was to him, she wouldn't bother. He loved the curls, the freckles, the spitfire attitude. Even when it was directed at him.

Apparently giving up, she let her hand drop with a shrug, smiling as she skipped toward the truck.

His chest tightened at her toothy grin.

Hell, he had it bad.

"Sorry about that. I had to put my sister in a chokehold," she announced as soon as she opened the door. Shoving her bag across the bench seat, she grabbed the *oh shit* handle and hauled herself into the cab.

Shane waited for her to get situated and buckled in before asking, "A chokehold?"

A sigh preceded her. "Yeah, after several months of not

living under the same roof, three weeks of it has us at each other's throats."

"Dare I ask?" he asked anyway. Having no siblings of his own, he was curious about her family dynamics. Plus, he just liked hearing her talk, so the longer she did, the happier he was. "I'm going to hazard a guess you're talking about one in particular?"

Her mouth pinched. "Alex, of course. She's selfish, immature, and a right jackass on occasion. Don't get me wrong, she's also brilliant, witty, and beautiful—and she wants everyone to notice." She cocked a brow at him. "Especially men."

Yeah, he got that. "I noticed."

"Oh, you want a chokehold, too?" Her eyes narrowed to slits.

Jealous, was she? He could live with that. His grin was lopsided when he placed his hand, palm up, on the seat between them. She laced her fingers with his, and a soft hum of energy vibrated up his arm.

"I already belong to a Winther," he said, gently squeezing her fingers. "She's kind of salty and laughs like a braying donkey, but I'm smitten."

She stared at him blankly. For a second, his pulse stalled. Then her lips curved into a smile that had his eyes crossing. "You shut up right now."

He threw his head back with a laugh. "Wow, someone needs to teach you how to flirt."

"That *was* me flirting."

Grabbing the gear shift, he put the truck into drive, then gave her a wink. "I know."

He debated turning on the radio but decided against it. Since he finally had her alone, he wanted to enjoy the time without the buffer of anyone or anything else— even music.

"How is living in the house?" he asked, regarding her from the corner of his eye. The one other time he'd been inside had convinced him it was no ordinary brick and mortar. Whether it was spelled or possessed, the place had a mind of its own.

Despite being deserted for over twenty years, there wasn't a cobweb in any corner. No dust on the mantel, no creaky, warped boards on the staircase. Hell, there weren't even weeds in the yard. It was as if the place had an invisible caretaker. Keyword, *invisible*. No one had been seen coming or going since Paul Winther had left in the middle of the night two decades prior.

Until Evie walked up the porch steps and the front door swung wide open.

He'd considered himself a man firmly rooted in the logical, physical world. No longer. Ten minutes in that place, and he'd nearly screamed like a spooked toddler.

"Strange yet, familiar. Sort of."

When he glanced over, she shrugged. "The house... recognizes us. Or, at least me. I'm not sure if my sisters have noticed the little things it does, but I do."

Fascinated, he wanted to keep her talking. "What little things?"

Her frown was pensive. "I have yet to receive an electric bill—thank God because I'd probably pass out—but we have power. The temperature is always 'just right,' ya know? Also, my bedroom door locks behind me when I leave."

He raised a brow at that. "Slanted floor?" Easily responsible for a door shutting on its own. And they'd only been in the house a little over three weeks, so the electric bill could be en route.

She shook her head. "I hear the lock click into place. When I reach for the knob, it unlocks. I had Elle try to open it." Her lips curved into a cocky, satisfied grin. "It wouldn't."

He snorted. "What about their rooms? Do they lock you out?"

"I don't know. I haven't tried."

"What?" Did he sound incredulous? Because he was.

"Why not? I'd be trying everything in that house."

"Yeah. But... what if it's just me?" she asked, finally meeting his eyes. "What if I'm the only witch?"

He cringed. That did pose a problem. While society had taken a hard turn at politically correct, witches—or casters as they preferred to be called—weren't a protected minority. They weren't even a minority because they weren't 'real.' Most people did not believe in witches, and those who did, were either friend or foe—there was no in between.

He was merely a guardian—a human who could see auras but had no power—but he wouldn't want to announce it to the world either.

As much as he hated it, Shane understood her hesitation. Especially since neither Alex nor Ellery had the same vibrant aura that Evangeline did.

Then again, he hadn't seen one around Evangeline until she came into her power. Perhaps her sisters were late bloomers.

"We'll figured it out together," he promised, reaching across the seat to rub her arm. She shivered at his touch, but he didn't think it was in pleasure.

.

Chapter Two

After Shane dropped her off, Evangeline walked into work with pep in her step and a smile playing on her lips.

She pulled up short at the amount of people in the library.

Carrow, her best friend in Whisper Grove, caught her eye and motioned her over, extricating herself from a group of kids. "One minute to spare, chica," she said, letting off a low whistle. "If you were late on your first day back, I think Mimi would have replaced you with the new girl."

"What new girl?"

Her shoulders lifted. "Some college kid Mimi hired to head the children activities."

Evangeline shuddered. It wasn't that she didn't like kids. She just... didn't like kids. Sure, they were cute—some of them—but they were also obnoxious, germ-carrying rebels. Basically, chaos in human form. Being in charge of one, much less a group of them, would take her to the second or third level of hell. "She must be a saint. Why are there so many kids?"

"I'm assuming you mean *here,* as opposed to in general. Please don't make me explain how they're made," Carrow said, voice dry.

"Oh, aren't we funny today?" Evangeline strolled past her to the office so she could log in. She wasn't officially working until she clocked in.

"I'm funny every day. You clearly need to pay more attention. As for the high number of little people, it's October," Carrow stated. As if *that* somehow explained the minors.

"Do children multiply in October?" They really were little gremlins, weren't they? Evangeline clicked the app to log her time, waiting for it to load.

"The parade is coming up at the end of the month. Kiddies want spooky stories, and their mommies want to research their costumes." Crossing her arms, Carrow sat on the edge of the table. "Happens every year."

"Parade?" Evangeline asked, scrolling through the hourly options.

31

"The Halloween parade. Are you kidding?"

"Uh, no. I've never heard of a Halloween parade." Unlike Carrow, Evangeline hadn't grown up in Whisper Grove. She had her suspicions as to why, but she'd never know for sure now that her parents were gone. Shaking off the maudlin vibes that came with remembering her mom and dad, she asked, "A parade, huh? With floats and marching bands?"

"One band, and it kinda sucks, but it's what we're working with. It starts with a parade, but more or less turns into a block party all the way down Main Street, from your house to the mayor's mansion. Ghouls, goblins, music, dancing—think of it as a rave with candy instead of drugs."

Evangeline laughed at the description. It actually sounded fun. She loved Halloween, as did her sisters. Maybe the parade would be a festive way to join their new community.

Mimi's ample form filled the doorway. She was covered in the brightest dayglow pink muumuu Evangeline had ever had the misfortune of seeing. "It's good of you to show up, Evangeline. Did you have a nice vacation?" Mimi stared down her nose, meaty fists planted on her even meatier hips.

Her tone, not to mention the outfit, chafed Evangeline's already-raw nerves. She finished her log in and signed off, then slowly stood. Several responses rolled through her mind, and she nearly settled on, *Oh, yes, burying empty coffins because my parents' bodies were burnt to ash was such a great time. Can't wait to do it again*.

A small part of Evangeline wanted to watch Mimi squirm. But giving in to the childish whim would make her the shitass, wouldn't it? Instead, Evangeline smiled. "I'm glad to be back. I think returning to my routine will help a lot."

As would watching you tumble down a flight of stairs, you vicious harpy.

Her response earned a sour scowl from Mimi. Evangeline smiled. It was the little things.

Not breaking eye contact, Mimi returned her smile. Evangeline stood up straighter, her alarm bells ringing.

"A kid barfed in the Early Reader section."

Carrow shot straight up from her perch, then practically ran from the office. "Oh, God, look at that shelf. I gotta fix it."

"I hate you," Evangeline shouted after her. Eying her boss, she crossed her arms. "You're really going to make me clean that, aren't you?"

"Who else would do it?" Mimi's painted brows arched.

Evangeline bit her tongue, reminding herself she loved her job. Usually. But right now, she hated her boss and was dangerously close to suggesting the evil woman mop up the floor with her ghastly outfit as it looked as though it'd already been barfed upon.

Rather than let her temper say something she'd regret, Evangeline left her boss smirking as she headed toward the supply closet.

Catching Carrow's eye on the way, she gave her a curled lip. Not that she expected Carrow to volunteer for clean-up duty, but why did Evangeline always get the crap jobs around here? Mimi hadn't even glanced at Carrow when she bolted out the door because her target was already in the crosshairs.

Why did the woman hate her?

Sighing, Evangeline chose the items needed from the closet, then went about the disgusting chore of cleaning up someone else's mess.

Reason number 471 to dislike children—they vomited.

Reason number 472 to dislike children—they didn't clean up their vomit.

Scrubbing complete, she tossed the paper towels in a separate garbage bag, double knotted the end, and threw it in the trash. After, she set the mop outside to be rinsed with a hose, then put the disinfectant spray away. Somehow, she'd managed not to throw up mid-chore, but now that it was done, her gag reflex was getting a serious workout.

"I love my job," she muttered under her breath.

After Evangeline finished putting everything away, Mimi snagged her to go through the books that patrons had ordered online from another library, to get them ready for pick-up. She also had to send out email notifications to said patrons to let them know their books were ready.

She slipped into the familiar tasks with pleasure. Several people checked out their books, a few needed help finding where a particular genre was shelved, and still others were searching a particular title.

She had never appreciated the mundane tasks more than now.

A loud bang rattled through her bones when Mimi dropped a stack of books on the counter. Evangeline jumped with a yelp, turning to see what had exploded.

"These need shelved," Mimi stated. Turning away, she added, "In the basement."

"Oh, yeah, no." Evangeline braced one hand on the counter, the other on her hip. Under normal circumstances, she would never, *ever* tell her boss to shove it—she had just cleaned up some kid's barf, hadn't she? But the basement was a strong and unequivocal *Up Yours*.

"Excuse me?" Mimi's frown was genuinely perplexed.

"Been there, done that, have the psychological trauma to prove it. I will no longer do the basement." Nervously, she bit her lip, but she was determined to stand firm. If Mimi wanted her in the basement, the woman would have to hogtie her and toss her down the stairs.

Mimi stared... It wasn't a glare so much as squinted confusion. Her beady eyes darted around the room, probably to make sure no one had witnessed Evangeline's defiance.

Carrow had—she was standing motionless in the center of the floor, watching them with interest.

Evangeline's stomach clenched. The last thing she wanted was a showdown with her boss, especially in full view of everyone. Choosing a different but equally honest tactic, Evangeline offered, "I'm sorry, Mimi. I don't want to be difficult, but I cannot go into the basement. It..." *speaks to me*. Not something she wanted to explain. "Scares me."

The dazed expression melted. "What are you—four? The basement freaks everyone out. Just get it done." Mimi waved her off.

Then, *There's something wrong down there,* flittered through Evangeline's mind.

Frustration snaked up her spine. She stretched to her full height of five-foot-ten, which was impressive, and glared at the shorter woman. "If you feel like something is wrong with the damn basement, then why would you send me, especially after I told you how *I* feel?" she demanded.

"What?" Mimi's eyes widened. She bowed forward, making Evangeline bend the other direction, and hissed, "I didn't say that."

"But it's how you feel," she said. "I can—"

"Whoa, ladies." Carrow was suddenly at Evangeline's side, gripping her arm to tug her away. "Let's not get *witchy*, m'kay?"

She was on the cusp of telling her friend to stuff it—that she hadn't brought out her witchy yet—but said friend's pointed look bore into Evangeline's skull like a drill. She sucked in a deep, calming breath, using the seconds to get a grip on her temper.

Carrow hesitated, then let go and focused on their boss. "Let's not forget that Evangeline has just suffered a great loss. She's just not herself yet. I, on the other hand, love all things dark and spooky. I'll shelve the books."

Mimi rocked on her heels, glaring down the slope of her nose. Evangeline thought for sure she'd press the issue, bracing herself to go home jobless.

Panic slowly squeezed her lungs. Losing her job when it was just her was scary, but with three sisters to take care of? Unemployed for four was terrifying.

Still, she wouldn't enter that basement. Not *ever* again.

"Fine. Make sure it's done properly," Mimi said, then she was stalking away.

Evangeline slumped against the counter, relief like a cool stream in her veins.

Carrow whirled on her, face tight. "Are you nuts? You do *not* reveal yourself to normies, much less where another caster might see you. Never. *Ever.*"

After the stress of the confrontation, it was several seconds of blinking stupidly before Evangeline realized what Carrow had said. Licking her lips, Evangeline pressed in close and whispered, "Do you know what I am?"

"I can smell my own, can't I?" Carrow crossed her arms. "Before you ask, no, you don't smell. I'm the same as you. I told you as much at the beach."

"You made a half declaration as you jumped into the lake," Evangeline protested on a shout.

Several patrons craned their heads around. She bared her teeth. Giving them her back, she sidled closer to Carrow. "You also said you were kidding."

"Well, yeah, you looked like I'd force-fed you a road apple. You weren't ready."

Evangeline sputtered, glancing around to make sure no one was eavesdropping. "Ready for what? Do I have to sacrifice a virgin to a pagan god? Bathe in goat's blood while dancing a jig under a full moon?"

Okay, so maybe she *was* shouting. Or maybe she just had the look of someone who was about to lose their shit in a colossal meltdown. Did she seem like she needed more stress? More responsibility? More effing confusion? No, she needed a quiet island off the coast, but she didn't inherit *that* dream, so she was stuck with these crazy heifers.

Snatching her by the arm, Carrow dragged her into the hall. "You need to get *control*—of yourself and your power."

"And how am I supposed to do that?" Evangeline asked in an equally vehement tone. "I don't know how to control it. I don't even know what the hell it *is.*"

Silently, Carrow scrutinized her from top to toe. Evangeline was about to ask what she expected to find, but Carrow blurted, "You need to see the Mitch."

Uh… m'kay. Not the announcement Evangeline had anticipated.

"I'll bite—who is Mitch?" she asked, rubbing her

temples. This was getting ridiculous. "And I need to see him, why?"

"You'll see. Tomorrow night, I'll pick you up around eight. It'll give me a chance to check out the house."

Evangeline watched her friend waltz off as casually as if they'd made plans for dinner and a movie. She had never gotten the chance to ask Carrow what her power was—if she was actually a witch. Did she have the same ability as Evangeline, which was to hear shit she didn't want to, or was Carrow hiding something else under her pointy hat?

Shane bolted awake at the annoying trill. It took him a blink or two to realize it was the garage line ringing. He fumbled for the receiver.

"Carlson."

"Hey, this is Leslie over at WGPD. One of our officers blew a tire on Lune Avenue, the long stretch out by Mayes' farm? We need a pickup."

Only about half of the information registered. Rubbing a hand over his gritty eyelids, he nodded, then felt like an idiot when he realized she couldn't see the gesture. "Okay. Be right there."

"Thanks. I'll let the officer know you're on the way."

"Yep." He replaced the receiver, staring at it blankly for a second. Then he turned on the bedside lamp, grabbed the notepad and pen he kept next to it for such occasions, and scribbled down what he remembered.

Blown tire. Mayes farm.

If Leslie had given him any more information, his groggy brain couldn't recall it.

His gaze rolled to the red digital numbers on his clock.

Two. In the morning.

"Shit."

These calls were the one thing he hated about owning a garage with a tow truck—he was the one responsible for middle-of-the-night emergencies.

With a yawn, he shoved off his covers and slowly pushed to a stand. He stretched, added in another yawn, and ambled down the dark hallway to make coffee. He was awake enough to realize what he needed to do, but he wasn't alert enough to do it.

Coffee was a must to operate heavy machinery in the godforsaken hour of two AM.

After putting on the pot to brew, he shuffled to the bathroom, stripped, and climbed into the shower, realizing too late he hadn't given the water enough time to warm.

He suppressed an indignant howl. As soon as the water hit lukewarm, he lathered and rinsed as fast as he could.

By the time he was dried, dressed, and moderately conscious, the coffeepot beeped the end of its brewing cycle.

"Thank God," he said, grabbing his cell phone from its charger as he headed to the kitchen.

The lights were shining brightly when he walked in, and a burly man stood in front of the pot.

"What are you doing up?" Shane asked, grabbing a mug from the cupboard. Not waiting for Buff to move aside, he pushed in and poured the dark liquid into his cup.

His uncle grunted. "Phone woke me."

"Hell, if you're up, then why am I?" Shane stared into this cup, only then realizing he'd meant to fill the thermos so he could take his coffee with him. "Shit."

 "Won't be the last time." Buff reached over his head, pulled out the thermos, and set it on the counter. "It's your job now. I'm too old for this crap."

It was Shane's turn to grunt. Right now, he was too old for this crap, too. He filled the thermos, added a bit of milk, and then snatched the keys from the hook by the door. "WGPD called in a blown tire. Be back in about an hour."

Buff raised his mug in salute.

Shane's snorted. "Thanks," was his good-bye as he shut the door behind him.

The chill in the air helped wake him. By the time he climbed into the cab of the tow, he was alert enough to spell his name, maybe even to perform simple math. Thrusting the key into the ignition, he cranked the engine with a grumbled, "I am definitely too old for this middle-of-the-night crap."

The drive to Mayes Farm took less than ten minutes, but he didn't see the cruiser until he almost blew past it. His brows rose at the sight of the bumper sticking out of the ditch at a forty-five-degree angle.

Flipping on his lights to warn other drivers, he pulled past the car and backed in, lining the bed with the cruiser's bumper. Satisfied he'd be able to pull the wreck out of the ditch without much, if any, damage, Shane climbed out of the cab and headed to the back of his truck.

The driver's door creaked open, and the officer stepped out of the cruiser.

Shane pulled up short. "Dean?"

Raising his arm to block the flashing lights on the top of the two vehicles, Dean squinted. "Hey man, I wondered if it would be you or Buff to pull me out."

Dean Taylor was Shane's best bud, had been since middle school. Dean's family had made Shane an honorary member the second they found out he was an orphan being raised by his uncle. Adding Shane to the family had given the Taylors' three boys.

"Buff said he's too old for this crap. You all right?" Shane stepped closer, then clapped his friend on the back as he peered at the front bumper. Shane let out a low whistle. It was a mangled, crumpled mess. "Whoa, dispatch called in a blown tire."

"Yeah. The blown tire is what propelled me into the ditch," Dean admitted, returning the brotherly back patting before stepping aside.

"How fast were you going?" Shane asked, moving past Dean to peer into the car. The cabin appeared intact. No damage or deployed airbag, he was pleased to see. Those sonsabitches were not fun to replace.

"I had just pulled out to chase down a speeding car. As soon as I flipped on the lights, the tire blew. The wheel jerked, my tire caught the grass, and I hit the ditch." Dean snapped his fingers. "Over in seconds."

"That's a lot of damage for not much speed." Shane blew out a breath. "But I'm glad you're good, man. I'll take it to the shop, look it over tomorrow, and let you know what I find. Honestly, it might be easier to buy a new one."

"Thanks, brother. I appreciate it." Dean frowned at the mangled metal. "The department is already short on cars, so I'm probably gonna get chewed."

"Can't help you with that." Given how small the department was, they probably couldn't afford to replace a cruiser. But Shane doubted they'd like what he'd charge to fix it, either. "You may be on foot patrol for a while."

Dean's face dropped. "That's not funny."

Shane laughed, his breath turning to steam. "I'll do what I can. Let's get it on the rig, then I'll drop you by the station."

While Dean gathered his equipment and personal items from the patrol car, Shane crawled into the ditch and hooked the chain to its undercarriage. Once Dean gave him the all clear, he pushed the button to drag the car from the ditch onto the bed of his truck.

Within minutes, Shane circled around and was headed toward town. The police department and jail were located off Main Street, as were most of the small town's businesses.

He slowed as they approached Evangeline's house. The moon highlighted the turrets like it adored them, lending to the mysterious feel of the structure, but the rest of the home was dark as night.

"I hear you're dating the Winther girl," Dean said, nodding to the mansion as they drove past.

News traveled fast in Whisper Grove, especially when it was about a Winther. Shane tsked. "Small towns, gotta love 'em. Where did you hear that?"

"You know cops are plugged into the grapevine." Dean shot him a grin. "Just kidding. I ran into your ex."

"Freya?" Shane suppressed a tired groan. Just the

mention of her name made his spleen roll over. She kept popping up, bad-penny style. "I can well imagine all the nice things she had to say about Evangeline."

Dean chuckled as he reached to turn down the heat. "Is that her name? Freya would only refer to her as 'that Winther.' She's jealous. I think she wants you back."

A snort preceded his, "I sincerely doubt it. Until recently, we hadn't spoken in years, not since she dumped me. She wants something, but it has nothing to do with me."

Acid churned in his stomach because he suspected it had to do with Evangeline. Freya had popped back into his life almost in tandem with Evangeline. Why? There wasn't a cell in his body that believed Freya was interested in rekindling their cold relationship his young heart had thought was a romance. No hitch in her stride when she'd cast him aside for her high-society man from New York.

Which meant, at least to Shane's paranoid mind, she was sniffing around him because of his girl. The only reason he could come up with was that Freya knew Evangeline was a caster. But how?

A guardian was supposed to be able to recognize someone with magic, but he couldn't tell if Freya was a caster or not. She was a witch, but was she a *witch*? Aside from Evangeline and her friend Carrow, Shane had yet to run into another, so he wasn't experienced enough to tell.

"Let's get together soon, man." Dean slapped Shane on the arm, dragging him into the present. "I'm off this weekend. Why don't you come over for the game? Bring pizza. I'll have beer."

"Yeah." Shane nodded, liking the idea of chilling with his buddy. Also, pizza and beer. "Sounds good."

"Cool." Dean gathered his gear as Shane pulled up to the curb. The police station was lit from one end to the other. "Oh, and I want to meet this lady of yours. She must be something to have Freya's claws out."

Shane had yet to meet anyone who didn't bring out Freya's claws at one point or another. It was sort of a rite of passage with her. He nodded his agreement, then said his good-byes as Dean climbed out.

As his friend disappeared into the station, Shane stayed at the curb a few minutes, letting everything Dean they'd talked about sink in. He really didn't like that Evangeline was on Freya's radar. Freya shouldn't even be thinking of his girl, much less discussing her with others.

That Freya was left a bad taste in his mouth and a sinking feeling in the pit of his stomach.

Something was coming, and it wouldn't be good for his witch.

Pulling away from the station, he decided discovering what Freya was up to topped his priority list. Whether it was petty jealousy or rival witches—which he still couldn't wrap his mind around—he needed to know, to prepare. To do that, he had to learn this guardian gig from top to bottom. That meant confronting his uncle and demanding answers, whether he wanted to give them or not.

Chapter Three

Evangeline snuggled deeper into the soft throw, curling her legs under her bum. Her knees ached from sitting for so long, but she didn't want to stop reading.

Every time she opened her father's journal, she felt closer to him. Unfortunately, she was no closer to understanding what he'd written. Still, flipping through these pages eased the lonely isolation she'd felt since her parents' death.

Her free hand snaked out from under the blanket, grabbed her cup, and then brought it to her lips. She took a sip, then grimaced at the cold coffee. Setting the mug aside, she turned the page.

Today I learned what it is to truly fear for another's safety. We haven't heard from Rachel since Monday morning. This evening, three days after she went missing, an officer came to our house to tell my mother they'd found my sister's car approximately thirty miles outside of town.

Her belongings were still inside, and the door had been left open. Rain had soaked the interior. Her keys were in the ignition, her purse on the passenger seat. And while there had been no sign of a struggle, I can't help but think she didn't get out of her car willingly.

Where would she go? Thirty miles south of Whisper Grove is nothing but farmland and forest.

The detective made the mistake of suggesting she may have left of her own accord. I thought my mother would make him swallow his tongue. Despite her insistence that Rachel wasn't the kind of girl to run away from home, I could see he didn't believe her.

No doubt many a mother has said the same to him only to discover later that the child had in fact left by choice.

But what the staunch detective doesn't realize is that Rachel isn't like others—none of those who have disappeared are.

Every missing person from Whisper Grove over the last three months was a caster.

Of course, no one can point out the obvious to a normal, that casters don't leave a safe community unless there is a very compelling reason. And even then, at least in Rachel's case, they wouldn't abandon family.

Rachel, as all the others, had been taken. I'm sure of it.

Which begs the question—who is strong enough to overpower a witch?

Not a normal. Unless they knew exactly what each witch was gifted with, and knew how to combat that power, they wouldn't stand a chance. A group of them? Maybe, but still, the odds are not in their favor.

The only thing powerful enough to attack and defend against a witch is another witch.

That truth sits heavy on my heart. The casting community is tightknit. We don't turn on our own. To think one, or more, might be harming our kind terrifies me.

Normals do enough damage... but a caster? That is much harder to fight, especially when we have no idea who the traitor might be.

After the detective left, me, Claire, Jolie, and our parents cast another locator spell. I don't know why we thought it might work this time when it hadn't the times before, but we sensed nothing of Rachel. Not only could we not locate her, but we also couldn't sense her life at all.

I think that was the moment my parents and sisters realized we would never see our Rachel again.

Evangeline sucked in a shaky breath. Even if she hadn't known she was reading her father's journal, she would have recognized him in the writing. His voice sounded in her mind with every word.

Because she'd studied the book front to back and over again, she even knew the locator spell he was referring to since he'd written it at the back. She didn't understand how a compilation of words worked magic, but her father obviously did.

Heaving a breath, she placed the journal on the side table and stood with a groan. Her muscles protested after sitting so long. She was stretching her arms overhead when a figure moving toward the stairs caught her attention. Expecting to see Alex, she opened her mouth to call out, but the words died on her lips.

She was too startled to do anything but stare.

Unlike her statuesque sister, the figure was petite. Her curly blonde hair was cinched in a low ponytail that draped down her back. Her flowy lavender skirt swished with each step.

She disappeared around the corner.

"Mama?" passed Evangeline's lips on a rasp. Her legs trembled as she hesitantly followed.

The foyer was empty. Still, she stepped through the archway into the foyer, turning to peer in every direction. She would have seen if her mother had gone into the kitchen, which left the door beneath the stairs or up to the second floor.

The instant she considered the door, a low hum drifted into her awareness. She shook her head. *God, please, not now.* If the whispering started up in her own home, she'd run screaming into the streets.

As quickly as it had begun, the vibration stopped.

Evangeline eyed the door. She had tried it several times already, but it never opened for her. Why would this time be any different? Approaching slowly, she wondered what she'd do if it *did* open. Exploring on her own didn't appeal to her, but curiosity pounded in her chest.

Her fingers were stiff as she gripped the cold knob. She pressed her lips tightly shut so she wouldn't scream. At least, not outwardly. Before she could think better of it, she twisted.

It was locked.

Her mother's perfume lingered. Evangeline sucked in as much air as her lungs could hold. Tears welled behind her eyes. Heart pounding in her chest, she glanced to the stairs, her gaze tracing the curved bannister to the second floor.

Taking the steps two at a time, she rushed up the

staircase. As soon as she hit the landing, the familiar click of her bedroom door unlocking made her hesitate. Was her mother in her room, waiting for her? Or had the door unlocked simply because she was near?

Her grip on the knob was shaky. She twisted, then released it with a soft push. The door creaked open, and Evangeline slowly crept into the room.

No Mom. No sweet scent of her perfume.

A door shut somewhere else in the house. Evangeline scrambled into the hallway, surveying each bedroom door. The second floor boasted four suites—one at each corner of the house. The front two, where the turrets looked out over the street, belonged to Ellery and Mallory.

She and Alex occupied the back two.

Evangeline focused on the room directly across the hall. A sliver of trepidation snaked up her spine. Logic stated her mind had played a cruel trick on her, that she'd mistaken Alex for their mother.

Her rational brain agreed. After all, Alex was blonde, slender, and at home. Of course she'd seen Alex. It made sense.

Her gut begged to differ. Her mama was smaller, more fine-boned than Alex. Evangeline had inherited her mother's unruly curls. And damn it, she would recognize her mom's scent anywhere.

Alex's bedroom door was ajar, just enough for Evangeline to see a crevice of light from inside. Forcing her reluctant body to move, she crossed the hall. Her heart tried to rise up her throat as she knocked on the door.

Nothing.

She pushed the door inward just as Alex stepped from her closet.

They both let out startled screams.

"Evie!" she yelped, clutching a sweater to her chest. Straightening from her spooked crouch, she added, "You don't like people to sneak up on you. Don't do it to me."

Normally, Evangeline would love a laugh at Alex's expense, but her brain was having trouble understanding what had happened. She *saw* her mom.

"I'm sorry, Alex. I thought—" She stared at Alex's clothes—a lavender maxi skirt with a white V-neck tee. Sadness spread through Evangeline's chest as she bit down on her lip to keep from wailing her grief. She'd been so sure she'd find her mother in this room, but she was mistaken.

"Evie."

Her gaze jerked to her sister. Swallowing her despair, she forced a jovial smile she didn't even remotely feel. "Sorry, I, uh, wanted to know if you've seen Chester today?"

Chester could hump a Pitbull for all she cared. That damn cat came and went as he pleased, ate his weight in tuna, and left black fur all over the place. She gave no shits about where he was or what he was up to.

Alex shrugged. "No. Why?"

Evangeline's phone rang. She hadn't even realized she'd grabbed it when she followed... Alex, apparently.

"Excuse me," she said, grateful for the excuse to retreat to her own room. Evangeline sat on the edge of her bed, staring at the screen.

Carrow.

Swiping to accept, she lifted the phone to her ear. "Hi."

"You have plans tomorrow night. Be ready."

"What?" Her scowl would leave permanent wrinkles. She rubbed her forehead.

"It's not easy to get everyone together, woman. You don't already have something going on tomorrow, do you?"

"No. What sort of plans?" Evangeline asked, perplexed.

"Tutelage. I promised to take you to Mitch, or did you forget?"

"I remember. I just didn't realize this clandestine conversation was an invitation to meet him."

"Her," Carrow corrected. "I hate to put it off until tomorrow, but I have things. Wear dark clothes. I'd put that hair up, too. It's distinctive."

Evangeline pulled the phone away to glare at it. "I'm sorry, are we in an episode of *Cloak and Dagger?*"

Carrow's long-suffering sigh drifted through the speaker. "This is how we do. If you want to go it on your own and hope for the best, be my guest. If you want to learn to control the power inside of you, then do as I say. What part of 'being discovered could get you killed' don't you understand?"

Well, when she put it that way…

"Sorry. I'm not exactly pre-disposed to stealth and secrecy."

"You'll get used to it. I'll be there by seven. Be ready."

"You said eight before," Evangeline shouted, but Carrow had already hung up.

"And you're standing on the edge, face up, 'cause you're a... *natural!*"

Shane cranked the volume, bellowing to the newest release of one of his favorite bands. What lyrics he couldn't remember, he made up and sang along to tempo.

Traffic was light on the way to town. He was returning to the shop after dropping a clunker off at the junkyard. The owner had asked him to take a look at it a month ago, then decided it wasn't worth his dollars to fix it. Nor, apparently, was it worth his effort to retrieve the damn thing from Shane's lot. After repeated calls, asking the owner to pick it up, Shane had left him a final voicemail threatening to turn it in for cash if he didn't call back.

Much to his surprise, the owner had returned the call and told him to turn it in, burn it, leave it—he didn't care. So, Shane delivered the largest lawn ornament in his lot to the junkyard. And was paid to do so.

His cell rang. He turned down the radio before pressing the answer button on his steering wheel. Technology was great, wasn't it?

"This is Shane."

"Hi," Evangeline answered softly. With that one word, she sounded lost. It was almost timid, as if she weren't sure about calling him.

Frowning, he took a left onto Main Street. "Hey, sweetheart. What's wrong?"

At first, there was only silence, and worry revved his heartbeat. "Evangeline?"

"Nothing," she said with a laugh that sounded forced. "I was wondering if you wanted company tonight?"

Did she even need to ask? "Of course. I can make you dinner," he offered, then cringed. His best dish was spaghetti, and it wasn't all that great. Maybe he could pick up some French bread or a salad or something? At least make it look like an adult meal.

Being just him and Buff, and both being no more gourmet than Chef Boyardee, cooking often took a backseat to microwavable dinners, cold-cut sandwiches, or takeout.

"As long as you can stomach overcooked spaghetti in a moderately acceptable sauce," he warned.

"That sounds nice," she said absently.

Something was definitely up. No one heard 'overcooked spaghetti and acceptable sauce' and thought nice. He got the impression he could've offered Alpo and Captain Crunch and gotten the same enthusiasm.

"What's going on?" he asked, his nerves telling him something was definitely wrong. "Are you okay?"

Her sigh was dismissive. "I'm fine, really. I'd just like to get out of the house for a while, and you're the only place I want to go."

Her confession put a smile on his face. "I can live with that. I actually passed your house a few minutes ago. Want me to swing by and pick you up?"

"No, I have a few things to finish up here first. Can you give me forty-five minutes to an hour?" she asked, sounding more like herself.

"Sure. I'll have dinner waiting on you. See you then." He disconnected, feeling rather pleased with himself as he pulled into his shop's parking lot. With the promise of his girl on her way, he was grateful to have the rest of the night free. Sometimes, Buff would book him past closing because the old man liked money rolling in. Especially when he wasn't the sorry sod bent over an engine block anymore.

Even though the weather was cooling, Shane had spent the majority of his day in the warm garage and had the B.O. to prove it. He sure as hell didn't want to present a crap spaghetti *and* body odor.

A shower was calling his name.

"What has you grinning ear to ear?" Buff asked as Shane stepped out of the tow. "You win the lottery, 'cause I could use a vacation?"

Slapping his uncle on the back, Shane answered, "In a manner of speaking. Evangeline is coming over for dinner tonight."

Buff crossed his arms like the surly jackass he could be. "I'm not making dinner."

"Since I'm not trying to chase her away, I appreciate that," Shane said dryly. Then added with a grimace, "I'm making spaghetti."

Buff's cringe matched his own. "You sure you're not chasing her off?"

"Be nice to her." After Shane entered the office, he placed the tow truck keys on the hook above the desk. He always did that first thing, or he'd shove them in his pocket and God only knew where they'd end up.

Buff had lost the other set years ago. Any thinking man would have a spare or two made before he lost the original, but neither Shane nor his uncle had made the effort. They'd no doubt kick themselves when the inevitable happened.

Glaring through the doorway, Buff announced, "I'm always nice."

Shane stilled, raising a brow, and his uncle straightened with an offended, "I'm not *mean*."

Letting silence answer for him, Shane slipped past the grump, patting his shoulder on the way. Buff's grumbled, "I'll eat in my room," had Shane laughing.

He turned on his heel, walking backward toward the garage bay. "You can handle one meal. Would you mind closing the garage? I need to hit the shower."

Buff shooed him off.

Shane trudged up the gravel drive to the house, his mind working over how to impress his girl with a basic dinner. His steps faltered. Why on earth was he making dinner? He should have picked up something that wouldn't taste like wet rubber tossed in marinara sauce. Checking his phone, he realized there was no time to implement that plan. In the time it would take him to go and return, she would arrive to better-tasting food but a foul-smelling boyfriend.

Sighing, he finished his walk to the house, making a beeline for his bathroom. After a quick shower, he dressed, brushed his teeth, and headed downstairs to start dinner.

He scoured the cabinets, searching for the large pot he

used to boil the spaghetti. Depending on which of them cleaned it last, it could have been shoved into the Lazy Susan by the stove, a cabinet next to the sink, or even in the pantry with the chips. Finding anything in this kitchen was a treasure hunt in which no one wanted to participate.

"There you are." He grumbled at having to remove a Doritos bag before pulling the pot from the pantry. Shaking his head, he filled it with water and set it on the stove just as Buff came through the front door.

"Why do you insist on putting pots in the pantry? You know that's for food, right?" Shane asked.

Buff's shoulders lifted. "Fits better in there. I'm taking a shower," he said, disappearing into his bedroom at the end of the hall.

Shane shook his head at his uncle's back. Pantry, Shane could live with. But if pots and pans started showing up in the coat closet or the garage, he'd have to put his foot down.

Busying himself with the sauce, Shane gathered four tomatoes, two peppers, and an onion. He dug a pan out of the cabinet it actually belonged in and set it to medium on the stove before drizzling oil to let them heat together.

He went about slicing and dicing the vegetables, content to get lost in the familiar recipe. He had just finished chopping the onion and adding it to the pan when a deep rumble sounded. Pausing, he cocked his head to listen.

From the low, steady hum, Shane figured the engine was a well-tuned machine. Drying his hands on a towel, he moved around the counter to peer out the front door window.

His mouth fell open.

A cherry-red vintage Mustang was creeping up his driveway. He hoofed it out to the porch, wondering who the hell was going to step out of that badass car.

To his shock, Alex Winther sat, seemingly perfectly at home in the driver's seat. She waved, and he numbly lifted his hand in response. When his girl stepped out of the passenger side, he practically leapt off the porch

"What year is this, and holy hell, where have you been hiding this bad boy?" he asked, running his fingers along the hood. This car was a beast.

"*Her* name is Rosita. She's a 1969 Fastback. Isn't she gorgeous?" Alex asked, eyes full of pride as she watched him like a hawk.

"She sure is," Shane murmured.

Evangeline sidled around the hood to join him. Bumping her shoulder into his, she said, "I'm surprised she's letting you touch. Alex usually unmans anyone who breathes too heavily around her precious baby."

Immediately jerking his hand back, he shoved it into his pocket. "No breathing here."

Alex's snort was barely audible as she shifted into reverse. "You two kids have fun. I'll see you later."

They watched her back down the drive until she turned around in the garage lot. Once she hit the road, the roar of the engine echoed to his bones.

"You're drooling," Evangeline stated.

"I know." He turned to face her, his expression full of regret. "It's best to do this now before we get any more serious. I'm sorry, but I think I'm in love with Rosita."

Evangeline blinked, then let out one of her diabolical *snaughs*. It started as a ripping snort before melting into laughter. "Oh, honey," she cooed, brushing her fingers along his jaw. "I thought *I* was going to have to unman you there for a second."

He grimaced at the visual of her crunching his lug nuts. On that note... he smiled—mostly—and tucked her under his arm. "Are you hungry?"

"I am," she said, snuggling in close. Stretching up on tiptoes, she brushed her lips against his cheek. "Thank you for letting me come over tonight."

He tipped her head up. Her lips were warm and soft

against his, and when she shivered against him, he deepened the kiss. He could have kissed her until the sun rose tomorrow morning, but his uncle, ever the subtle suave creature that he was, hollered, "Shane, your damn sauce is burning!"

He let his shoulders droop with a putout laugh. "It's always something. Let's go in before I scorch dinner, huh?"

Her answering smile was so radiant his breath caught in his lungs. A soft glow permeated the air around her, and he knew without asking that she was content. Lacing their fingers, he guided her into the house, where the acrid smell of burnt tomatoes filled his nostrils.

"Oh, shit." Buff hadn't been kidding. Shane darted around the counter to peer into the pot. He let out a chuffed breath. Not his best sauce, but it was salvageable. Lifting his gaze, he shrugged. "I hope you like spaghetti topped with very well-done homemade marinara."

"It's my favorite," she said, shooting him a grin before removing her coat and hanging it over the back of the chair.

"That's why I adore you." He shot her a wink, delighted when she ducked her head to hide the soft blush spreading over her cheeks. Her aura deepened to a reddish orange.

"Oh, dear God, you two aren't going to do this at the dinner table, are you?" Buff marched past Evangeline to grab plates from the cupboard. At least he always put those in the same place. Placing them on the counter, Buff scrutinized Evangeline so long that Shane almost barked at him. But she took it, meeting his gaze with a steady one of her own.

Buff held out his hand. "We've never been formally introduced. I'm Shane's uncle, Buff."

"Nice to meet you. I apologize for bursting in the first time we met."

Shane cringed at the memory. The night she'd found out her parents were killed in a house fire, Evangeline had shown up on a hunt for answers about her family. Since he hadn't been expecting her, he'd had notes, newspaper clippings, and old photographs of her family and several other witches who had gone missing spread across the counter.

She'd accused him of stalking her, of orchestrating their first meeting—even though she'd plowed into him— and then dashed out the door before he could explain.

Buff's lips pinched tight. He gave her one jerky nod. "Not necessary. You needed answers to questions that probably still make no sense."

"That would be a huge understatement," she stated with a wry smile.

Shane poured the simmering sauce into a bowl, taking care to leave the charred bits in the pot. He hoped it didn't taste like burnt butt. After draining the noodles, he added them to a separate bowl and set it next to the sauce. Not for the first time, he wished he'd picked up some bread.

Or Chinese takeout.

"Dig in," he said. "It's going to taste worse the longer it sits here."

Shane waited for Evangeline and Buff to fill their plates before doing the same. Though they had a dinner table just a few feet away, they settled around the island.

"I expected much worse," Evangeline stated around a mouthful of noodles. "Given the smell and all."

"Are you tasting this? What could make it worse?" Buff asked. He cocked his head. "Maybe roadkill?"

"Both of you get out, right now." Shane shoved a sloppy forkful into his mouth. "You don't need to abuse the cook."

"Need to—of course not. Want to? You betcha." Scooping up a glob of noodles, Buff saluted Shane with them. Then he surprised the crap out of Shane by asking, "So, Evangeline, how do you like the house?"

Shane froze with his fork midway to his mouth. Buff wanted nothing to do with witches, casters, power, or anything that might remotely resemble magic, which he'd been professing since Shane had met Evangeline. Since the house clearly had its own vibe, Shane couldn't believe Buff had even brought it up.

"Umm." She licked her lips, put her fork on her plate, and then folded her hands. "It's lovely. It definitely has its own personality."

"Uh-huh. No doubt about that." Buff sat back and regarded her. Shane wondered not only why his uncle had asked, but also what was he hoping for?

"You knew my parents well?" Evangeline asked.

Shane couldn't say why the conversation put him on edge—he was as curious as she was—but he felt like he was sitting at the edge of a cliff in a wind storm and, any second, something would blow him over.

Buff took the time to wipe his mouth on a napkin, fold it neatly, then set it down before answering. His big head nodded slowly. "Very well. What would you like to know?"

Shane's mouth dropped open. Who the hell was sitting across from him? His uncle was tight as a snare drum with him, but Evangeline asked one question and was a Q and A free-for-all? Crossing his arms, Shane leaned back in his seat and waited.

"Who were they?" She drew a deep breath. "I've known

them all my life. Yet, they feel like strangers to me now."

"They were good people. Kind people." Meeting her gaze, he added, "Powerful."

Evangeline leaned forward. "My dad—was he like me?"

"A caster? Of course."

She shook her head, her gaze flicking to Shane. "No, I mean, did he hear things?"

"Oh." Buff relaxed in his seat. "Here's the thing about casters—they're secretive about their gifts. Even guys like us, guardians, who can see the power around them, we can't tell what that power is." He softly added, "The only caster who shared her power with me was Jolie."

"My dad's sister." She paused, then asked hesitantly, "Would you be willing to tell me what her gift was?"

Buff seemed to consider this, then shrugged as if it wasn't killing him inside. "I don't see what harm it will do now. She called it *The Wishing*."

"Wishing..." Evangeline spoke softly, tasting the word on her tongue. "What exactly is that?"

"Illusions." Buff suddenly stood, his chair scraping loudly across the tile floor. He grabbed his plate, carried it to the sink. "It's a tricky gift."

"Illusions, like a magician?" A frown crinkled her brows. "Like if I wished to see someone, I would... if I was around someone who had that ability?"

"Sure," Buff agreed. "Once Jolie mastered it, she could make anyone see whatever she wished them to see."

"I thought it was the house playing tricks on me, but I wonder..." Evangeline murmured.

"What do you mean, the house playing tricks on you?" Shane asked. And why was this the first he was hearing of it? "What happened?"

"That house was built with the blood of the first Winthers, created to protect that bloodline. It won't play tricks on you. In fact, that stone monstrosity is one of your greatest assets."

Buff's revelation eased some of the knots in Shane's gut. At least when home, Evangeline was safe. Now, if the rest of the world would fall in line, he'd sleep much better.

She smiled absently, and Shane rapped the table with his knuckles to get her attention.

When she glanced at him, he raised his brows in question. But rather than answer, she said, "If I could ask one more thing before you go?"

Buff's shoulders drooped. He had the countenance of a man who wanted to lick his wounds.

"Maybe another time," Shane offered.

"No, I'd rather do it now," Buff stated, leaning on the edge of the counter. "Go ahead."

Evangeline opened her mouth, hesitated, then blew out a shaky breath. "There are four of us, just like my dad's family. Since I'm a witch, does that mean my sisters are as well?"

"I've never contemplated the genetics of it." Buff's surprise showed. "Since Paul was a caster, it's likely at least one more of you would inherit power, if not all, but Lily wasn't, so it's a possibility you stand alone."

Evangeline deflated. Her gaze dropped to her hands. "That's what I was afraid of."

The mood shifted from conversational to contemplative as they cleaned up dinner and put away leftovers, which would most likely get dumped. After Buff said his good-byes, he retreated to his room.

Evangeline picked up the dish sponge, then cranked the faucet. "Soap?"

"You're not doing the dishes," Shane said, reaching around her to shut off the water. He took the sponge, tossed it in the sink, and then pulled her close with his hands on her hips. "I want you to tell me what happened."

She cocked her head. "What do you mean?"

He gave her a *really* look. "When you asked to come over tonight, something was wrong. And unless my keen detective guardian skills are misreading it, whatever is bothering you is related to the questions you were asking my uncle."

A slight smile played on her lips. "Your skills are keen indeed," she said, wrapping her arms around his waist and resting her head on his chest. She released a slow exhale, and the heat of it seeped into him.

He curled around her. The soft scent of her shampoo filled his head. God, she smelled amazing. "Do you want to tell me about it?"

"I saw my mom today."

Whoa. Shane couldn't say what he'd expected, but Evangeline seeing her dead mother wasn't it. He could imagine the shock. Keeping his tone neutral, he asked, "Did you speak to her?"

"No. I saw her from the corner of my eye as she started up the staircase. I was sitting in the living room, so by the time I got to my feet, she was gone."

Her body was shaking. He rubbed her back and arms, trying to stop her trembling. When his efforts did nothing, he pressed tighter against her, attempting to physically stop her shivering.

"Did anyone else see her?" Sensing she was on the

verge of a breakdown, he wanted to keep her talking.

"Alex was there, but I don't think she did." She lifted her head to peer at him with a steady gaze. "I *saw* her, Shane. It wasn't my imagination."

"I don't think you were imagining her, honey. I believe you."

Her lip quivered. She nodded before returning her head to his chest. Not knowing what else to do for her, he stood there and held her, letting her take what she needed. If she wanted to talk, he'd listen. If not, there was nothing wrong with the comfort of silence.

She let out a jaw-cracking yawn. He grinned into her hair. "I'm starting to think all of your involuntary noises are over the top. I live in terror of the idea of—"

"Don't you say it," she commanded, jerking her head up. "Women do not fart."

"Fart?" His brows shot high. "Honey, I was going to say your stomach grumbling."

"Sure you were," she groused before letting off another yawping noise.

Glancing at the stove clock, he was surprised to find it was pushing ten. They'd talked for three hours? It was amazing how fast time went when he was with her.

Resigned to an end to their night, he crooked his finger

under her chin and tipped her face up. "Do you want me to take you home?"

She peered at him from under her lashes. His pulse skidded to a halt. Curling her fingers around the nape of his neck, she pulled him down to her. "No," she murmured against his lips. "I want you to take me upstairs.".

Chapter Four

The front door clicked at her approach. Her lips curved with appreciation. Not that a house anticipating her arrival wasn't incredibly weird, but it was also kind of nice.

Especially after a wonderful night of no sleep.

As Evangeline passed through the open doorway, her family's familiar cacophony of breakfast noises slammed into her. Scrubbing a hand over her face, she set her purse by the fireplace before pushing through the swinging door into the kitchen.

All motion stopped as her sisters stared.

"Well, well, look what the cat dragged in from a night of carousing," Alex said, lifting her coffee cup to her lips. The mug hid nothing of her smirk, which Evangeline figured was how she wanted it. "Never thought I'd see you do the walk of shame."

"And I never thought you'd be awake to see it. I'd hardly call spending the night at my boyfriend's carousing." Evangeline sat at the empty seat across from Alex, then pointed a finger at Elle, then Mal. "Which neither of you will do until you're twenty-five."

Mal stood and collected her dishes. "I don't have time for boys," she announced. After dumping the dishes in the sink, she left the kitchen.

"She gets that from you," Alex pointed out. "I've always made time for boys."

"Yeah, we know. But she gets dumping her dishes in the sink for someone else to clean from you."

Alex rolled her eyes. "Whatever. At least Elle shares my appreciation for the male of our species."

"Oh, no, I'm not getting in the middle of this." Elle made like her twin and bolted, mumbling something about being late for school.

Evangeline craned her neck to check the coffee level in the pot. Surprised to find it only half empty, she jumped up to retrieve a cup, poured in her cream and sugar, and then filled it to the brim.

One sip and she was on her way to feeling human.

Granted, one cup wouldn't pull her out of zombie mode after so little sleep, but her world righted itself with each additional sip. "What's on your agenda today?"

Alex sat her mug on the table. "I figured I'd see if anyone is hiring."

"Oh, that's a great idea." Evangeline's surprise must have shown because her sister's lip curled in response. Softening, she added, "It wasn't an insult. I would just appreciate some help with money. Besides, a job would give you the chance to get out and meet people."

"I suppose you're right," Alex agreed on a sigh. "I definitely need to get out of this house."

Evangeline nibbled her lip. "Is the house..." *giving you trouble?* That sounded stupid. And weird. Clearing her throat, she went with, "I mean, do you like it?"

Not much better.

"Oh, it's gorgeous, don't get me wrong. And I do like it. It's just... different." There was an odd resonance in Alex's tone. It vibrated through Evangeline, and she couldn't help but wonder if her sister's words were an evasion of some kind. Not a lie, per se, but not the truth, either.

Alex cinched Evangeline's certainty by dropping her gaze to stare fixedly at the liquid in her cup. An evasion on any level was very un-Alex-like.

As much as she wanted to jump in head-first and ask Alex if she was experiencing strange things in the house, or more importantly, if strange things were happening directly to her, Evangeline had less than an hour to get ready for work, which was not near enough time to delve into all the weird they'd inherited.

The possibility Alex hadn't seen or sensed anything held Evangeline back as well. If she listed all the strange ways the house responded to her and Alex gave her blank stare, or worse, laughed at her...

No thanks.

Even with the suspicion that Alex was like her, a witch, Evangeline couldn't bring herself to ask. Did it make her a coward? Perhaps, but she preferred the word practical. Why step into a pile that might turn out to be shit when she could step over it?

Having finished her coffee, she rinsed the cup and set it on a towel to dry. "I have to get ready for work," she stated on her way out of the kitchen. "Good luck with your job hunt."

Alex mumbled thanks as Evangeline climbed the stairs. The door unlocked before she reached the top. "Can't get one over on you, can I?" she muttered.

Chester's soft meow pulled her to a stop. He wound his slinky body through her legs, rubbing against her shins.

"Speaking of carousing all night, where have you been?" she demanded. Her mood was definitely java improved, or she wouldn't have reached down and scratched the cat behind his ears, earning her a rumbling purr.

A smile curved her mouth when he flopped onto his side with satisfied sound. "Unfortunately for you, kitty boy, I don't have time to rub your belly."

Stepping over him, she cut through her bedroom on her way to the shower. One of the best things about this house was that they each had their own master suites. They would never have to share a bathroom again.

Stripping out of her clothes took her mind back to her night with Shane. He'd been sweet and gentle, but her body ached in the most delicious ways. Her mind replayed some of her favorite parts as the water splashed over her skin.

Though he hadn't said it since the night her parents died, she knew he loved her. She heard it in his voice, felt it in his touch, and in the way he held her. And while she still wasn't ready to say it aloud, she loved him.

When her world started to spin out of control, she found herself turning to Shane. Everything realigned when she did. He was the rock that anchored her. As long as she had him, everything would turn out fine.

"You might let her read the journal."

The scream tore from her chest. She scrambled to cover herself before she realized the words had sounded in her head—a small consolation, given who they came from. Ripping open the shower curtain, she snarled at the culprit sitting in her bathroom sink.

"Chester, get your dirty ass away from my toothbrush. And get out of my bathroom!"

His terror was so great he merely licked his paw and ran it over his head.

Growling, Evangeline grabbed the shampoo bottle and hurled it. It landed with a clunky thud several feet off the mark, but the damn feline darted off the counter and out the door.

"Ha!" she gloated at his scrambling backside.

Victory was hers.

Except her shampoo was across the room.

"Damn cat," she groused, darting out of the shower to grab the bottle, then hurrying back in before she dripped water all over the floor. It would be just her luck to skid into the splits as she stepped out of the shower.

Nothing quite as fun as starting a long shift with a crotch rip.

"House, don't let that furred fart in my bathroom again,

okay? Can we make a deal for that?"

The house remained silent.

She continued her litany of insults, questioning not only Chester's morals, but also his origins. Why did she keep that cat, anyway? Oh, right, because he came with the house. Was it even possible to send him packing? He'd only find his way back. Besides, her sisters would welcome him with open arms and cans of tuna. They adored the wretch.

Heaving a steamy sigh, Evangeline admitted she couldn't live with evicting him since she did—*almost*—like him, too. But damn him to hell and back before she'd let him know it.

What had he been doing in her bathroom, aside from scaring her hair straight?

Oh yes, something about letting Alex read Dad's journal. *Ha*. Evangeline would rather exfoliate her face with his kitty litter than arm Alex with her deepest, darkest secret.

 Obviously, the cat had distemper.

Then again, if Alex discovered the truth through Dad's words, it wouldn't reveal Evangeline's secret. If Alex wasn't a witch, she'd only think Dad had lost his marbles.

Shame on Evangeline for her willingness to sacrifice

their dad's reputation, but she'd forgive herself.

Perhaps Chester wasn't as rabid as she'd thought.

Evangeline rinsed the shampoo, slapped on the conditioner, and then washed her body. Now that she'd decided to share, she was anxious to do so.

She dried as fast as she could without performing any involuntary calisthenics on the slippery tile floor, then rushed to dress, her pulse pounding in her ears. She was dying to know Alex's reaction.

Retrieving the journal from under her mattress, Evangeline skipped down the stairs, catching Alex at the bottom before she climbed them.

"Hey," she all but shouted, making Alex jump in the air. "Oh, sorry. I was thinking about what you said the other day."

Alex scowled. "That you're a bore?"

"Very funny. No, about Dad's journal." Evangeline thrust it into her sister's chest. "I want you to read it."

With little choice but to accept the book, Alex leveled a questioning expression on her. "Why?"

Here we go.

"You need it more than I do right now. I think it will give you the answers you're looking for. Just promise me you won't let the twins see it."

Another frown as Alex lifted the cover. "Why?"

Evangeline gently placed her hand over the top, keeping her from opening it. She waited until Alex met her gaze. "Because they're not ready."

For the first time, Evangeline tried calling her power. It responded immediately, and the familiar soft static sounded around her. "Promise me?" she asked.

Alex regarded her for so long that Evangeline worried she wouldn't. Finally, her sister dipped her head in agreement. "I promise."

The words sounded as clear as a sunny, cloudless day.

Joy bubbled from Evangeline's mouth. Alex's frown deepened, but she didn't care. Her power had answered when she called. Because of it, she heard the truth—her sister would keep the journal to herself. For the first time since Evangeline's power came knocking on her door, she was delighted to have it.

"Great. Oh, when you're done, just put it on my bed, okay?"

Cocking out her hip, Alex asked, "How? You always lock your door."

Which Alex wouldn't know unless she'd tried to sneak in. Even that couldn't bring down Evangeline's mood.

Grinning, she poked Alex on the shoulder. "Caught you, heifer. Stop trying to get into my room."

Alex shrugged. "Old habits."

Evangeline snatched her purse by the fireplace, crossed the foyer, then paused with her hand on the front door. Turning her head, she said, "I don't lock the door. The house does."

Then she walked out, the door shutting itself behind her.

Evangeline came home an hour late, tossed her purse by the fireplace, which had become its resting place, and headed straight for the kitchen. Chester darted between her feet to beat her through the door.

"If there isn't leftover coffee in that dang pot, there will be hell to pay," she grumbled.

Mimi had given her a list of chores to complete before she left. If there had ever been any doubt the woman had it out for her, it had dissipated like a stale fart in a stiff wind.

She'd unboxed, shelved, reshelved, unshelved, boxed, wiped down, and taped up more books today than all the days of her life combined. Her back ached, there was a pinch in her neck, and her left eye was twitching to the beat of the *Macarena*. Oh, and she had sprained her pointer finger.

But hey, she hadn't had to clean up poop, pee, vomit, or crusty boogers, so the universe had smiled on her. A drunken, leering one, but a smile nonetheless.

Pushing through the swinging door, she found Ellery making a sandwich.

"Hey," she greeted, moving to grab a cup from the cupboard. "Is there coffee? Tell me there's coffee."

She wouldn't make it through half an hour with Carrow and this mysterious Mitch without a serious influx of caffeine.

"Hey, yeah, I think there's some left from this morning." Elle nodded at the half-full pot. "Where have you been? I thought you'd be home an hour ago."

"Being worked to death by an evil taskmaster. I swear that woman is plotting a death-by-books end for me." After filling her cup, Evangeline took a long drag of the dark liquid and gagged. Not only was it cold, but it tasted like a coal miner's socks. Placing the cup in the microwave, she debated how long to nuke it. Hot socks were better than cold.

"I'd give it a minute," Elle said around a bite of her

sandwich. "Anything less will only warm it, which is almost as bad as cold."

She had a point. Punching the number, Evangeline then turned and leaned against the counter. "Where is everyone else?"

Specifically, Alex. Evangeline glanced toward the door as if she could will her sister to walk through it.

"Mal went for a run. I think she's in the shower now. Alex has been locked away in her room since we got home from school."

Evangeline couldn't keep her brows in check. "*Mallory* went for a run?"

Mallory Saffron Winther went to running like ketchup went on popcorn. Evangeline shuddered.

"Yep." Elle smirked around another mouthful. "I thought the same thing. Must have had a rough day."

The microwave dinged. Evangeline removed the cup, making hissing sounds as it burnt her fingertips. Rather than wait for the cup to cool, she grabbed another from the cabinet and poured the liquid gold into it.

"I'm going out with Carrow tonight. I'll leave money on the mantel for dinner. You guys can order pizza or something."

Elle nodded. Evangeline backed out of the kitchen, took

the stairs, then turned right at the landing. Another right at the end of the hall brought her to Alex's room. She knocked lightly. "Alex?"

No answer.

She rapped her knuckles again, harder this time. "Alex, are you in there?"

Nothing.

Evangeline stepped back to peer at the crack under the door. Light shone through from the other side. Was she in the bathroom? With a sigh, Evangeline started to retreat when Chester's paw poked through and curled around the bottom edge of the door.

"How did you get in there?" she asked, reaching down to lightly scratch his paw. It disappeared with an offended growl.

Deciding she didn't have the time to coax him from Alex's room, she retreated down the hall to her own. As always, her door clicked and swung inward. She shook her head at the oddness, even more at how quickly it had gone from odd to normal, and set her coffee on the dresser.

After stripping out of her work clothes, she peered into her closet. "What does one wear to meet a witch named Mitch?" A snort trailed the lame limerick. Dear God, she was going to end up in the looney bin before this was over.

She chose a pair of jeans and an NC State sweatshirt she'd gotten in college. It wasn't exactly the dark clothing Carrow had instructed she wear, but after the day she'd had, Carrow was lucky Evangeline kept the bra and didn't opt for sweatpants.

She chugged the coffee, brushed her teeth, and pulled her hair into a ponytail. A quick peek in the mirror later, she declared herself ready. Her gaze darted to Alex's door as she left her bedroom. Still closed. Not that she'd expected to find her sister waiting in the hall, but she was anxious to see her reaction to the journal.

Evangeline headed back downstairs. She retrieved a couple of twenties for dinner and was setting them on the mantel when a knock came from the door.

Elle peered in from the kitchen. "Oh," she said, a hint of surprise in her voice. "I didn't realize you had come downstairs."

"Just did. Money for dinner." She pointed to the bills, then walked to the door and let Carrow in.

"Hey, girl!" Carrow bounced into the foyer, full of energy and good cheer. She was definitely decked out in spy wear—black pants, black shirt, black cap on her head, and her hair in a single braid hanging down her back. The woman resembled an overgrown fairy jewel thief. She scanned Evangeline's outfit with a frown.

"Ready to go?"

Right after we poke you with a needle, hopefully deflate some of that effervescence.

"Yep," she mumbled, slinging her purse over her shoulder.

"You won't need that," Carrow stated, giving her purse a pointed look. "Unless you want to drag it around with you."

"Where are you going?" Elle asked.

Carrow's head whipped around, her braid nearly taking Evangeline's eye out.

"Jesus, woman, watch that weapon," Evangeline commanded, backing up.

Did Carrow show concern for her eyeballs, apologize? Hell, no. The chit ignored her for Elle.

"Hi, I'm Carrow. You must be…" She nodded slowly. "Ellery. Yes?"

Elle's eyes widened. "Yes."

"Thought so. You have that color." Carrow took Elle's hand in her own, placing the other one over the top of their clasped hands. "Hmmm, interesting one, aren't you?"

"Huh?" Evangeline asked, fascinated despite her

confusion.

"I'm taking big sis here to meet some friends of mine. Won't be long." That was all Carrow said before spinning on her heel and waltzing toward the door.

"Money on the fireplace." Evangeline waved to her sister, then rushed after her friend.

Carrow was waiting for her at the gate. "She's interesting, your sister."

"What do you mean?"

"She's colorful." Carrow shrugged. "Not what I expected."

"What the hell does that mean?" Evangeline followed her to the car. "What aren't you telling me?"

"Lots of things," Carrow admitted with a laugh as she motioned for Evangeline to get in. "Coming?"

Blowing a raspberry, Evangeline climbed into the passenger seat. "You know I don't like it when you're evasive."

"It makes you cranky."

"Yes, very cranky. So who is this Mitch?" she asked, connecting her seat belt.

"You'll see."

Evangeline let out an exasperated huff. "That's not an answer."

"Sure, it is." Carrow grinned, cranking the engine. "It's just not the one you want."

Evangeline was totally unprepared for her to peel away from the curb as if Satan were scouring the streets for a fresh soul.

"Jesus!" Evangeline snagged the 'oh shit' handle a second before Carrow took the first left on two wheels, slamming her against the door. "Where's the fire?" she hollered over the squealing tires.

The car immediately slowed to a normal speed. Carrow patted her leg. "Sometimes it's good to get the blood flowing."

"And the pee? Because I'm almost certain I just did." Evangeline knew it wasn't her colon emptying, because the poor sonofabitch was still sitting back at the curb. She returned the leg patting with more force, adding a pinch for good measure. "I think I tasted my spleen, too, you shitass."

The lunatic threw back her head, howling with laughter. Evangeline couldn't help but notice Carrow didn't bother to look at the road, and she almost pushed the hyena's hands aside to control the steering wheel herself.

"Now that you got whatever *that* was out of your system, where the ever-loving hell are you taking me?"

The direction they were headed took them past Shane's house. A few miles beyond that was all farmland for miles. Pretty much any direction from town was farmland. Unless this Mitch was a dairy or hog farmer, she couldn't imagine where they were headed.

Carrow cleared her throat. "The Brew."

Evangeline's mouth made a sound like a kicked donkey. "The Brew? That's the other way." She hitched her thumb back toward her house.

"I know!" Carrow stomped on the gas once more.

Carrow mapped the streets of Whisper Grove for another half an hour. She'd putter through town, and then, as soon as they hit an open road, she'd turn into a long-lost Andretti and burn rubber.

Evangeline had screamed herself hoarse fifteen minutes ago, which was probably for the best since she couldn't clamp her mouth shut to keep from barfing and scream at the same time.

Finally, Carrow pulled up in front of Wicked, the bar next to the coffee shop, and parked. Turning in her seat, she gave Evangeline a sympathetic smile.

"I really do have a reason for putting you through that."

"You were a Kamikaze in another life?" Evangeline asked through her nausea. "It would serve you right if I yacked all over your seat."

"Try to control yourself," Carrow warned.

"Control *myself?*" Evangeline gaped. "This, coming from you?"

Carrow laughed. "Two things before we head inside. One, I did that to get your energy up. Our gifts are controlled by our emotions, so the more out of control you feel, the more your power makes itself known."

"You couldn't have just yelled *boo*?" Unbuckling her seat belt, Evangeline turned sideways in her seat. "Or, I don't know, warned me?"

"No. I need you agitated so I can see what you project into the world when you're upset." Carrow gave an uncomfortable shrug. "It also tells me how strong your power is."

"And?"

"Later—I promise. Two, from the minute we enter The Brew, you must not speak. At all. Do you understand?"

"No." Evangeline threw her hands up. "Who in their right mind could? Are you taking me to an occult leader? Am I to be a sacrifice?"

95

"Hardly. Wait—are you a virgin?" Carrow asked, a mischievous glint in her eye. She must have noticed the murderous intent in Evangeline's because she lifted her palms in surrender. "Just kidding. Geez. And for the record, I'm taking you to the elder of our coven."

"Coven? Like, witch coven?" Evangeline asked, stupefied it might actually be a thing. "You're kidding. Right?"

Carrow shook her head. "Just remember what I said. Radio silence until I say so."

Evangeline was still trying to make sense of everything she'd said when Carrow climbed from the driver's side. Evangeline peered through the windshield, debating whether she should wrestle Carrow for her keys and get the hell out of there, or follow blindly—and mutely—as her daffy friend expected her to do.

Sighing, she opened the car door and stepped out. With a slight push, she made the door swing shut. "Since we're not inside, I want it noted I'm doing this against my better judgement."

"Noted." Carrow took off toward the small coffee shop, leaving Evangeline to follow and wonder why she hadn't parked in front of The Brew instead of Wicked. No one else was parked in front of the coffee shop. Surely she had noticed when she'd chosen her spot.

Whatever. She'd learned Carrow did what Carrow did,

and there was no rhyme or reason to it.

When Carrow reached the shop, she paused, peering in at something on the other side of the glass. After a few seconds, she nodded. "Remember," she said, placing a finger against her lips before opening the door and stepping into the shop.

Evangeline did as instructed, keeping her mouth shut as they took the last spot in line. The barista glanced up at the bell. He was young, probably late teens to early twenties, with sandy-blond hair and light blue eyes. His jaw was sharp, his cheekbones high, and his blue eyes full of intelligence.

Was it her imagination or did he falter when he spotted Carrow? Their eyes met, held, and then he gave an almost imperceptible nod before returning to his task.

Carrow reached out, then grabbed Evangeline's hand. The shock of it almost had her asking what she was doing, but Carrow squeezed hard enough to shut her up, then pulled her out of line. Together, they made the short trek down the hall to the rear of the store. The door at the end was marked *employees only*, but Carrow pushed right through, revealing the inner workings of the shop.

Questions bubbled up. Evangeline mentally popped them to keep silent. Carrow tugged her out the back door, pausing only long enough to make sure it latched shut behind them. Lifting a finger to her lips, Carrow led her around the corner of the building and into an alley. Thankfully, it was as short as it was dark because the streetlights didn't shine brightly enough to reach the narrow path.

Evangeline wondered what sort of things she'd see if they had, but then banished the thought from her mind. Ignorance was the better option. After the alley, they skated down a dim residential street. Though there were streetlights, Carrow surreptitiously avoided them, winding through one shadow to the next until darting in between two small bungalow-style homes.

She paused only to glance back the way they'd come before crouching low to creep forward.

Evangeline was dying to know what the ever-loving stupid they were up to, but to open her mouth now would be like admitting defeat. Besides, with all the secret-squirrel spy shit, she was more curious than ever to see where this adventure took them.

Like the third floor of the Dorothea Dix Mental Hospital.

Carrow straightened behind a house that appeared to have a gray-green siding. It was hard to tell the exact color under the moonlight. She surveyed left and right, then released Evangeline's hand with a look that warned her to remain silent.

Carrow lifted her arms into the air, swaying back and forth as she twirled her hands in circles.

What is this hocus pocus shit? Evangeline nearly threw in the towel right then and there.

But something caught her eye. Cocking her head, she stared at the spot on the wall, certain her mind was playing tricks on her.

The siding cracked before her eyes Yet, it happened without a single sound.

Evangeline jumped. Her head whipped around to Carrow, but she was staring intently at the same spot on the wall. The splintered slabs slowly pulled back along the house, and Evangeline realized they were sliding apart to reveal a hidden staircase leading down into darkness.

Before she could express the *holy shit* coursing through her veins, Carrow jerked her head toward the cellar-like stairs. Like, the crazy bitch wanted her to go down them.

This time, Evangeline was perfectly comfortable expressing herself. "Not a chance in hell." She crossed her arms. Watching Carrow's every move, her limbs tensed for a fight. "You tell me what's down there."

"Answers," Carrow stated, then rolled her eyes. "I have to close it behind us. Stop at the top if you have to, ninny."

Evangeline definitely wanted answers, but damn right

she was a ninny. The only friend she really had in this place had just dropped some serious magic mojo at her feet. And without warning, she might add. Evangeline had no idea that sort of thing was possible, much less that her quirky, geeky friend could pull it off without a crack in her broom.

Still, she'd come this far, right? It wasn't as if she was going to run into the night back to her house—because she wasn't entirely sure which direction it was. Grumbling her discontent, Evangeline crossed to the top step and notched her chin high, her eyes daring Carrow to call her on it.

"On more," Carrow ordered, clearly annoyed. "I need to be inside, too, you know?"

"Fine." She descended one stair.

"Jesus," Carrow muttered, turning toward the entrance. She magic-wanded her hands again, and the sliding slipped back into place.

"I'm going to have nightmares about this," Evangeline hissed into the near darkness. Thank God there was a light somewhere below, illuminating enough for her to descend without breaking her neck.

"It's the protection spell making you antsy. But, eh, maybe one or two nightmares," Carrow agreed, squeezing past her to bound down the rest of the stairs, as swift and sure as if she'd done it a hundred times.

Then she disappeared around the corner.

Oh, piss on that.

"Carrow?" Her voice sounded tinny and small in the tight staircase. The answering silence set her pulse racing. *"Carrow."*

A soft light flickered from another room. "Come on already."

"Come on already," she mimicked in a whiny voice, squinting to find each narrow step as she descended what was no doubt a level of hell. "You know I have a thing about basements, right? Driving like a blind bat, not letting me talk, holding my hand..." She griped her every complaint with each step. "Then deserting me on a dark, rickety staircase. This is all adding up to me strangling you with your pigtails, witch."

Finally, she reached the bottom. One deep breath later, she took the corner.

Chapter Five

Exhaustion clung to him, sticky as the sweat coating his skin. It might have been mid-October in North Carolina, but inside his garage, it was high noon in the Sahara. Even with the bays wide open, none of the cool air reached him. He'd been fantasizing about a cold shower since lunch.

After wiping down his tools, he put them away and cleaned off his work counter. He paused, his gaze skipping to his office as he debated whether to write up the invoice for Mr. Harrison before heading home or waiting until the morning.

Better to do it now while everything he'd done was still fresh in his mind. His legs were heavy and stiff, and his back cursed him a blue streak, but he sat at the desk and jotted down what he'd refilled, replaced, and removed. He'd calculate the total bill first thing tomorrow.

He shut the remaining garage bay, slid the bar into place that would make it impossible to pry open, then left through the door to the right of it. His keys jingled as he searched for the correct one on the chain. He slid it into the lock, turned until it clicked, then shoved the keys back into his pocket.

Though his house sat half a mile behind the garage, that short distance took forever. By the time he pushed through the front door, he didn't care about a shower. He wanted nothing but sleep.

Buff glanced up as Shane passed through the kitchen. "You want a burrito?"

"Sure," he said, heading straight for the couch. He sat with the groan of an old man, then snagged the remote off the table in front of him and pressed the power button. Whatever channel it was on was good enough for him.

"Rough day?" his uncle asked, setting a plate on the table in front of him.

"No, just long. Mrs. Perkins," Shane offered as explanation. Mrs. Perkins *was* the explanation. Sweet as the day was long—and they were really, *really* long when she came into the shop.

"Oh, Jesus, did she bring Alice?"

Shane was mid-bite in his burrito when he shot his uncle a *duh* look. "Has she ever not brought that damn dog?" *Alice*. What a ridiculous name for the canine version of the Terminator. The teeth with fur should have been named something more befitting her personality.

Like Cybil. Or Satan.

Buff sat in the chair next to the couch, mumbled something about Evangeline staying the night being to blame for his grumpiness, and started channel surfing. Shane tuned it all out. Thoughts of Evangeline had been the only thing that kept him from biting people's heads off all day. The softness of her lips when she sighed against his, her delicate curves pressed against him. Her scent had lingered with him all day.

Cramming the rest of his burrito into his mouth, he stretched out on the cushions, tucking an arm under his head.

Nah, she wasn't evoking any sort of crankiness in him. He blamed that damn dog. Listening to the thing's echoing bark for three hours straight—because Mrs. Perkins didn't believe in their convenient drop-off policy—had given him a pounding headache. It still hammered at his temple like an angry drummer.

Shane didn't know what she thought she'd accomplish

by watching his every move, but that woman was vigilant. And talkative. Dear God, could she talk. The mix of her high-pitched voice and Alice's yapping had convinced him he'd been a bad person in another life and karma had come home to roost.

His soul was still curled in the fetal position as his lids drifted shut.

The car careened around the corner on two wheels, sending his body crashing against the passenger door. Terror clutched his heart, cinching tight and setting his pulse to thrum in his ears. He swallowed with a dry throat.

"Jesus!" The name ripped from his mouth on a scream, but it wasn't his voice. A hand, also not his, grasped the 'oh shit' handle on the roof. "Where's the fire?"

Evangeline's howl was nearly drowned out by the screech of the tires as the car came to a dead stop.

"Sometimes it's good to get the blood flowing."

His head turned at the other voice. Evangeline's friend, Carrow, sat in the driver's seat, grinning back at him.

"I think I tasted my spleen, too, you shitass," flew off his lips.

What in the hell was going on here? He shook his head.

Except he didn't. Instead, he asked, "Now that you got whatever that was out of your system—and it'd better be out, or I'll set your hair on fire—can you please tell me where we're going?"

He'd have laughed, but he had no control of his body. Or Evangeline's body, apparently.

Shit was getting weird.

"The Brew."

His mouth fell open. "The Brew? That's the other way!" His hand jerked up, hitching his—hers, whatever— thumb toward the back of the car.

"I know!" Carrow hooted, and the car shot forward once again.

Shane had no idea how long she scorched the streets of Whisper Grove, but it felt like a century had passed when she finally brought the car to a slow, controlled stop. It was in such contrast to the way she drove, he wondered if they were hallucinating now.

"That was fun."

His stomach rolled, and he swallowed with effort. "It would serve you right if I yacked on your seat."

Shane agreed. All over it. The backseat, too. He couldn't even lift his hand to steady his spinning head. Whatever this connection was with Evangeline, he prayed to God there were no carnival rides in her future.

"Try to control yourself," Carrow warned.

"Control myself?" He gaped, indignation burning a hole in his gut. "This, coming from you?"

Carrow's laugh was as crazy as she was. "I did that to get your energy riled. Power is tied to emotion, so the more out of control you feel, the more your power rises."

"You could have just yelled boo!" His hand reached down and fumbled with the seat belt. Finally clicking the button, he turned in his seat. "You could have at least warned me."

"Oh, right. Should I have said 'I'm about to agitate you. Make sure to get upset.' Makes no sense." Carrow unbuckled, and then reaching for the handle, paused. "We're going into the Brew. You cannot say a word while we're in there. Understand?"

"No." Evangeline threw up her hands. "Are you taking me to devil worshippers or something? Am I to be your sacrifice?"

Fear pumped through him. He could feel that Evangeline was merely exasperated and using sarcasm to show her frustration, but he couldn't help but wonder what exactly Carrow was up to. Granted, he didn't know her well, and what little he did know was eccentric, so his judgement was skewed, but why the secrecy?

"Hardly. Unless...are you a virgin?" Carrow asked, a mischievous glint in her eye. Her hands lifted in mock surrender. "Just kidding."

Carrow climbed out, her laughter a tinkling sound that made them grit their teeth. Poking her head back in, she said, "Remember—radio silence." The door promptly slammed shut.

He, er, Evangeline, stayed right where she was, watching Carrow walk around to the sidewalk. Apparently, she decided—against his better judgment—that Carrow was safe to follow because she exited the car, shutting the door with a warned, "I want it noted I'm doing this under duress."

"Noted."

He was a passenger in her body as the two women made their way to the coffee shop. There was no denying he was curious to see what Carrow had up her sleeve, but another part of him didn't entirely trust her. Sure, she'd been a friend to Evangeline, but all this secrecy sat like an anvil in his gut.

And despite somehow riding shotgun, there wasn't a thing he could do to help Evangeline if things went awry. The impotence of the situation made him edgy.

They entered the coffee shop. Carrow immediately went

to the back of the line, which was only three deep. Neither spoke a word despite chatter all around them from the other patrons.

He noticed the kid behind the counter straightened when he saw Carrow. If Shane hadn't caught that small hitch, he wouldn't have seen the kid nod slightly before returning to his work.

What the hell was going on?

Carrow grabbed their hand, and a current traveled up his arm. Thankfully, Evangeline chose that moment to glance over. A soft light surrounded Carrow, and Shane realized that by touching Evangeline, she was including her in the energy.

But what was it doing?

Carrow pulled them out of the line. They walked to a door with an employees only sign and pushed through. The woman didn't slow or pause to look around—she knew exactly where she was going as she led Evangeline out the back exit.

She was a flashlight in the night with her aura glowing as it was, and Shane couldn't help but worry it would draw attention to them as they slipped into the shadows between two buildings. Carrow wound them up and down side streets, avoiding all forms of light—from streetlights to dim porch lights on the homes they passed.

Wherever she was leading, Carrow did not want to be seen. Shane couldn't decide if her stealth was a good sign or something he should worry over.

Whether it was Evangeline's blood pumping through her veins or his own nerves infiltrating their bond, Shane felt a lightheadedness slowly creeping up on him.

Their winding travels eventually brought them to a rundown home at the edge of town. From the looks of it, it had been abandoned since the dawn of time. Paint peeled off the sides. The left part of the porch was at least two to three feet lower than the right. Several of the steps were missing. From his vantage point, he saw two upper windows had been broken out. And none of that counted the graffiti kids had painted over it for years.

All in all, this was not the sort of place people on the up and up visited.

Skirting around to the rear of the house, Carrow finally dropped Evangeline's hand. His girl's relief flooded his senses, but he was still anticipating more weird shit and couldn't set his fears aside that she was in danger.

Without a word, Carrow ran her fingers along the wall, as if trying to locate something. Then she lifted her arms high above her head, her hands twirling in opposing circles. From one heartbeat to the next, the siding where she'd touched split and the two halves slowly parted. Between the moonlight overhead and the soft glow from Carrow, Shane could see a narrow staircase leading down to a dimly lit landing.

Oh hell no.

Everything in his body recoiled from the feeling he got looking into those shadows. There was someone—something?—down there he did not want a face-to-face with, and he sure as shit didn't want Evangeline down there.

Up until this point, he'd been a willing passenger, curious to see what his girl would see. Now, he put all his effort into reaching her. He yelled in her mind, tried to exert his control over her limbs, but when Carrow nodded for her to take the steps, his girl said it all for him.

"Not a chance in hell." She crossed her arms, stepping aside. "You tell me what's down there."

"Answers."

Shit. The minute the word was out, he knew she had Evangeline. She would descend those damn stairs, and there was nothing he could do about it. That she would do something so foolish infuriated him. Did the woman have no sense of self-preservation? Didn't she realize it would break him if something happened to her?

Apparently not, because she slipped between the parted slabs and started down the steps. He felt the splintered wood from the supports as she brushed her hand along the wall to steady herself. If not for the barely illuminating light at the bottom, she wouldn't have been able to see them at all.

His breath grew heavier in his lungs with each step she took. His thoughts swirled in his mind, becoming scattered, hard to hold on to. He remembered not wanting her to go into the darkness, but he couldn't for the life of him remember why.

The pressure on his chest intensified. The shadows blurred, and no amount of squinting and blinking cleared his sight. He couldn't catch a full breath. His connection to Evangeline started to slip, and he grabbed onto her, terrified that if he didn't stay with her, he'd never see her again.

As quickly as it had come, it left. The power stopped pushing against him, its weight lifting from one breath to the next.

Then something grabbed his heart, squeezing it, twisting and turning it with malicious intent. Shane struggled against the pain, certain his heart would be ripped from his ribs, but there was no way to fight back. He was powerless against the attack. Shane gritted his teeth in agony, hoping since he couldn't defend against it, he might endure it.

Evangeline's consciousness slipped over his, and he realized she'd reached the bottom of the stairs. He watched her turn the corner as his heart threatened to explode, fear helping the power kill him.

In the room at the bottom of the stairs was a group of women. They stood in a semi-circle facing Evangeline.

The last thing he saw before he was yanked out of her mind was a large snake, slithering its way across the floor toward the woman he loved.

Shane awoke with a scream. He clutched his chest as his body jackknifed, dumping him on the floor between the couch and the table.

"Jesus, Mary, and Joseph!"

His uncle's shout was nearly drowned out by the roar in Shane's head. He sucked in a lungful of air, relieved when the tightness in his chest slowly loosened. His blurry vision began to sharpen as the dizziness faded.

Suddenly, the table was jerked to the side, then Buff was on all fours next to him. Concern pinched his brows. "What the shit. You all right, son?"

Shane started to shake his head, but his gorge rose with a wave of dizziness. Stilling, he whispered, "Not so much."

"What the hell happened?" Buff helped him to his feet.

Shane immediately flopped onto the couch, weak and trembling. It was like he had a fever—cold sweats, aching limbs, and a dry mouth. Blowing out a stream of air, he counted to ten. Then he attempted to rise.

His legs buckled, dumping him on the couch. "Fuck!"

"Slow down, Shane." Buff dragged the table back to its spot, then sat on it, ignoring the crackly groan of protest from the wood. "Now, tell me what happened."

Shane pressed his palms into his eyes. "I don't know. I fell asleep, but then I was out with Evangeline and Carrow."

Buff relaxed, relief clear in his voice. "So, a dream?" He patted Shane's knee in reassurance.

"No." Shane scooted to the edge of the cushions. Even that small movement made him want to donate his burrito to Buff's lap. "I mean, I was *with* her. My body was here, but *I* was with her."

Buff regarded him in silence. "Like a dream walk?"

Shane's shoulders lifted. "I guess, maybe. Have you ever done that?"

"No. God, no." Buff scratched his head, then ran his palm down his face. "Are you sure it wasn't just an intense dream?"

A snort shot from Shane's lips. "If it was, it's the worst

one I've ever had."

He filled Buff in on what he saw and heard, how he couldn't control his own movements or voice. He explained Carrow's erratic driving that still made him want to barf, and how as soon as Evangeline entered the stairwell, something snapped his connection with her.

"Ah, hell, kid." Buff stood with a groan, then began pacing from one side of the living room to the other. "That sounds more like astral projection than a dream. And the fact that you were forced out?" His mouth pinched.

"She's in danger, isn't she?" Shit, he knew it. Shane glanced around for his phone, determined to warn her. Where the hell had he put the damn thing? Checking under and between the cushions, he considered what he should tell her.

"Not necessarily, but I don't like it. You said she was greeted by a group of women?" At Shane's nod, he let out a *hmmm*. "Covens are very secretive. Could have a simple spell to deter unwanted visitors."

"Carrow took her there," Shane protested. "She *was* wanted."

"But you weren't." Buff stopped before him, bent with effort, then held out the phone he'd picked up. "Fell on the floor when you were thrashing about."

Accepting the phone, Shane gave his legs another try. This time when he stood, they held, but they weren't as steady as he'd have liked. They shook like he'd spent the last three hours at a full run.

His walk was more shuffle on his way to the kitchen. After he dialed Evangeline's number, he pressed the phone to his ear as he rummaged for a glass. He filled it with water from the fridge while the other line rang.

"Please answer, baby." He just needed to hear her voice, to know she was all right. The glass was halfway to his lips when the line picked up. "Evie?"

Hi. I'm not available to take your call. Please leave a message.

Evangeline scanned the group of women standing before her. They returned her stare, silent and watchful. "You brought me to your book club?" she asked, lifting a brow at Carrow.

"Were you seen?"

Evangeline glanced to the woman on the left. She had soft caramel-colored skin and smoky green eyes. Her long black braids had begun to fade to a dark gray, which seemed to highlight the contrast to her complexion.

"Of course not. I know how to execute a cloaking spell, thank you very much." Carrow's head jerked toward Evangeline. "And I grabbed her hand, so she was unseen as well."

"That's why you held my hand?" Evangeline squeaked. "You made me *unseen*?" Was it her or were things spinning around the room? She glanced down at the lower half of her body expecting to see through herself.

Carrow scowled. "What did you think I was doing— making a move?"

Before Evangeline could admit she hadn't a clue what Carrow had been up to, the same woman peeled away from the group.

"In that case, welcome," she said with a voice as thick and smooth as honey, extending her hand. "I apologize for my rudeness. It's a habit to make sure no one was seen coming here. Carrow has told us so much about you."

Evangeline took her hand as Carrow said, "Mitch, Evangeline. Evangeline, Mitch."

The woman gave her a sympathetic smile. "My name is Grace. But you may call me Mitch if it suits you better."

Evangeline frowned. "Oh sure, Mitch and Grace are practically interchangeable, they sound so much alike."

Elbowing her, Carrow said, "Mitch stands for *mom witch*. Grace is our eldest and strongest caster. She watches over us, keeps us safe." She shrugged. "Like a mom."

"I see." Sort of. Not really. As Evangeline scanned the rest of the group, she realized there was a Hispanic kid who seemed as though he'd rather be anywhere but in the basement with a bunch of women. "Can I ask what you need protecting from?"

Grace clasped her hands in front of her, and Evangeline noticed she had a ring on every finger. Some were silver bands, some were gold. Others had stones and beads. Evangeline was fascinated by the collection. "From those who might wish us harm. Come," Grace said, motioning her forward.

Evangeline met Marie—a middle-aged Hispanic woman who barely looked up from her knitting to acknowledge Evangeline—and her son, Aiden. Aimiria, a blonde about Evangeline's age, and Sydney, Grace's daughter.

Though her skin was a shade lighter, Sydney was nearly a carbon copy of her mother. Same complexion, same smoky eyes, same vibrant smile.

Apparently, there were three others who were unable to make it tonight: Lennon, Holden, and Bonnie.

Sydney smiled. "It's nice to meet you, Evangeline."

"Thanks, you, too, though I'm feeling a little out of my league, especially with the daughter of the eldest. That must be a challenge to live up to," Evangeline said. Realizing it might have come across as an insult, she gave herself a mental kick. She wasn't usually so inept. Evangeline counted the night's strange events among her excuses. "Sorry, I didn't mean that to sound like it did."

"Actually, I'm only a spark, so I can't live up to it." Sydney laughed with the statement. "It's cool."

"Oh." Right. A spark. Evangeline was glad it was cool

even though she hadn't a clue what it was. "A... what?"

"A spark is a witch who cannot cast," Carrow explained, "Aimiria is one, too." She dipped her head toward the blonde. "They have power but cannot manifest it."

"Wouldn't that make you human?" Evangeline asked.

Aimiria stuck her nose up. "That's offensive."

"Ignore her." Leaning in, Carrow whispered, "She's always offended. Quick rundown. We come in all levels. As you know, guardians are the first step between humans and witches. They can see power, but have none of their own. Sparks..." Carrow paused to indicate Sydney and Aimiria. "Have power but cannot cast spells or manipulate the energy. Witches are those of us who can control the power. *But* we cannot see other casters like guardians can. It's a circle. We all need each other. That's why you are so lucky to have a guardian—most of us don't."

"You have a guardian?" Aimiria scowled. "Who is it?"

Carrow made a disgusted sound in the back of her throat. "Wouldn't you like to know? Oh, look, a cheese tray."

Her friend scrambled across the room to a small table in the back. From Evangeline's vantage point, it appeared to have an assortment of cheeses, fruits, and vegetables spread over it. Because a meeting of witches wouldn't be complete without a potluck.

Carrow lifted a carrot in question, and Evangeline shook her head. She'd been starving when she left the house, but the thought of eating now made her queasy. She blamed Carrow and her carnival ride here.

"Where's Bonnie?" Carrow asked around a mouthful of something. Her hands were equally full when she returned to Evangeline's side. The smell of the food filled her nostrils, making Evangeline want to slap the items out of her hand and look for a bucket to hurl into.

"You smell like warm cheese," she whispered. "I'm going to vomit on you."

Without a word, Carrow moved several feet to her right. "Where's Bonnie? I thought she was bringing the anchor?"

"I have it," Grace said, pulling something from the pocket of her long dress. She ran her thumb over the front before offering it to Evangeline.

Evangeline took it, her heart lunging into her throat. The stone was smooth at the back and polished flat. But on the top, it was carved with curving lines in a continuous circle. It was the same symbol that ran throughout her house. "What is this? This symbol is all over my house."

"It's your family's crest, for lack of a better word. This is the Winther coven's sigil."

"*Winther* coven?" The blood rushed to Evangeline's head. The room began to spin. Stumbling to the nearest chair, she dropped. She'd inherited a 'witchdom'? Gripping her head, she muttered. "Winther coven. Of witches. In the basement of a rundown, deserted house."

Grace's light chuckle kept her from passing out. For now. "You don't know much about who you are, do you?"

"Try not at all," Evangeline corrected. "Does anyone have some Xanax?"

She'd never taken the pill—or any meds of that nature—but she knew it was supposed to relax like nothing else. Given her current heart rate, she figured she needed something to calm her down before it exploded.

Choosing a seat opposite her, Grace sat, quietly situating the folds of her dress. "It's time you learn. Your—however many greats—grandparents, William and Elizabeth, were both immensely powerful. They realized it was only a matter of time before Salem turned on them like they had other casters, and they fled with their children and Rebecca, Elizabeth's sister, and her family.

The lights dimmed. Grace pointed to something behind

Evangeline. When she turned, she was shocked to find a movie-like projection on the wall. Grace's voice told the story even though she wasn't speaking.

Evangeline searched the source of the projection, but it appeared to come from nowhere. She spun her seat to face the wall, fascinated at the faces and places appearing in 3D before her.

"They made a home here, living peacefully with humans for many years. Though they didn't parade their magic around, they didn't hide it either. It was a haven for casters. Until dark symbols began appearing around town. Most humans didn't realize what they were, what they harnessed. But when their livestock and wild animals began to turn up dead, mutilated, and drained completely of blood, they put it together.

"A witch who wants more power must take it from other living beings.

"It started with animals, but it quickly moved on to humans. Fear spread, gossip ran wild, and your family knew if they didn't hunt down the caster using sacrificial magic, the life they'd worked so hard to build would be destroyed.

"What they didn't realize but would soon enough was the dark practitioner was one of their own—Rebecca. Naturally, poor Elizabeth couldn't stomach killing her own sister, so she banished her and her family."

The lights flickered back to full strength, and the vision dissipated like steam. Evangeline turned as Grace sat back in her seat. The elder let out a long sigh. "I'm sure you can guess where I'm going with this. Banishing did not stop the killing. Rebecca grew stronger, consumed with gaining more power. She riled up the townsfolk by spreading lies about witchcraft and sorcery, and pointing the finger at her sister.

"Long story short, they defeated her. Even somehow managed to convince the rioting humans that she was the threat. Everyone returned to their lives, and all was well. Until twenty-five years ago when dark sigils appeared and witches started vanishing. We've been in hiding ever since."

Grace's smile was sad when she stood and peered at Evangeline. "So, yes, you are in what appears to be a rundown house—to those who would avoid such a place. To those whom such a dwelling piques their interest, it resembles a well-maintained family home. Anyone who falls in between is kept away with a sense of unease created by our protection spell. Even with all of that, we come in cloaked."

Evangeline swallowed a lump of undiscernible emotions. Fear? Oh, yeah, check that box. Horror, anger, sadness? Those, too.

"I had no idea," she said, her voice barely more than a whisper. No wonder her father had fled in the middle of the night. As hard as it was to learn about everything now, she was glad her father had chosen to keep it from them. "On a side note, does anyone else find this insane?"

"Is it really so hard to believe? Carrow said you hear things most do not. Surely you know my words are true?"

"I didn't say I didn't believe you. I just find this to be crazy." Turning to Carrow, Evangeline asked, "How do you know about my power? I never told you."

Carrow popped a strawberry in her mouth. "How many times must I remind you that I'm awesome?"

Aimiria rolled her eyes with a low sound of irritation. Carrow stuck her tongue out.

Grace sighed like the tired Mitch that she was. "Carrow is the rare caster who can see other witches and their gifts."

Evangeline frowned. "Shane's uncle Buff said only guardians can see a witch's power."

"Normally, that's true. But like she said—I'm rare. I'm also a lean, mean, casting machine. Spells come easy to me." Carrow wiggled her brows, then shoved another piece of something into her mouth. Motioning for Evangeline to sit next to her, she said, "Shane and I see the same thing differently, though. He, I assume, sees the soft, rounded colors of a person's aura. I see the jagged, firm lines of power. It's the same energy, but I can figure out what kind by the way it spikes."

"So… you knew from the beginning?" Evangeline asked, a little miffed at the revelation. Had Carrow befriended her to be her friend or because she was a witch? She couldn't hide her scowl.

"No, actually, I only suspected with you. You were bound up tighter than a geisha. But when I heard your last name, I knew for sure. But Elle is rocking her gift. I saw hers immediately."

Evangeline straightened her spine clear to her brain. Unfortunately, her brain chose that moment to take a hiatus. "Elle?" she asked. "*My* Elle? She doesn't have power. Does she?"

Alex was the one she'd expected to be like her. Had she been wrong? Was Elle the caster? Or were they both? Pinning Carrow with a hard look, she demanded. "What is it?"

As if she'd been waiting for her to ask, Carrow leaned in and whispered, "She moves with the dead."

Chapter Six

Something smelled wretched.

Evangeline crinkled her nose at the stink. Pressing her cheek into her pillow, she tried to slip deeper into the dark recesses of sleep. Something tugged her covers. She tugged back.

"Evie."

No. This time when she yanked the covers, they came up and over her face. She slowly drifted back into dreamland.

"Evie."

Go away.

Whether she only thought it or spoke it aloud, the

sentiment was the same. *Be gone*.

Cool air stroked her cheek as the blankets were lifted off her face. She snatched it back, then jerked it over her head.

"Come on, wake up." Alex's annoyance penetrated the sleep-induced fog surrounding Evangeline's brain.

A ripe curse on the tip of her tongue, Evangeline popped out from her cozy nest, coming face to furry face with a set of twitching whiskers. And the source of the stench.

"Chester, you mangy feline," she shouted, pushing him away. The cat let out an offended yowl as he scrambled from her bed. "Stay out of here until you learn to brush your teeth like a civilized animal."

"What do you expect, feeding him a can of tuna every day?"

Evangeline squinted at the bedside clock. Her narrowed gaze slid to Alex. "It's six thirty in the morning. Is the house on fire?"

"No."

"Anyone bleeding?" she asked in a calm tone.

Alex smirked. "Not that I'm aware of."

"Then why the ever-loving hell are you in my room?"

Evangeline demanded, swinging the pillow at her sister's head.

Laughing, Alex ducked out of harm's way. Wrestling the pillow out of her hand, Alex tossed it back at her. "We're witches, Evie."

Evangeline stilled at the excitement in her sister's tone. It wasn't what she'd expected. When she regarded Alex, she saw none of the confusion and fear she'd fought through. In fact, Alex appeared downright delighted.

"That doesn't bother you?" she asked tentatively. She couldn't tell if Alex genuinely believed they were witches, or if she was only toying with her.

"No, I think it's amazing." Alex curled up next to her, tucking her hands under her chin. "After reading Dad's journal, everything made sense. It became clear to me. I'm *excited*."

Of course she was. Like most things in life, Alex sailed through where Evangeline had gone through hell. Between the whispers, the lies, and the talking cat, for shit's sake, she'd been ready to check into a psych ward.

Alex was beaming like it was Christmas morning.

Sighing, Evangeline reached for the glass of water on her nightstand. She took a sip, glaring at Alex over the rim. "If you were a bubble, I'd pop you."

"I want to cast some spells."

The water turned to ash in her throat. Evangeline choked and sputtered, spraying her mouthful over her bedspread. Wiping her mouth, she cranked her head around. "You what?"

"Look," Alex said, shoving Dad's journal at her. "There are a bunch of spells in here. I tried one, but it didn't work. I thought if we tried together, we could—"

"Stop." Evangeline took the book, placed it on the bed out of Alex's reach, then shoved it farther for good measure. "Slow down. Yes, we're witches, whatever that really means, but I don't know how to work a spell." When Alex started to object, Evangeline cut her off. "Why don't you go downstairs, make some coffee, *please*, and I'll be down in a few minutes?"

Mouth pinching in frustration, Alex made a show of snatching the journal before flouncing off in a huff. Evangeline gripped her throbbing head. Her gaze scrolled to the alarm clock. Six forty-five. Letting out a miserable groan, she flopped back onto the bed, then considered crawling under the comforter and blowing off Alex for another hour.

But she'd wanted answers when she'd found out, so no doubt Alex was gritting her teeth at the imposed patience. Evangeline forced herself out of bed. After a long, strange night with Carrow and her merry band of witches, she was not adequately prepared to face the day ahead on so little sleep.

"You had better have that coffee going, Alex, or so help me," she threatened to the empty room as she shuffled into the bathroom.

By the time she'd scrubbed and brushed the necessities, she was feeling less homicidal as she made her way downstairs. Alex had a cup of coffee on the table waiting for her. Said sister nodded with an encouraging smile for Evangeline to take her seat.

Gawd. She really wasn't awake enough for this yet. Not only that, but she also hadn't processed everything that had happened the night before—cloaking spells, anchor stones, and a frisking coven. Having seen it all with her own eyes didn't make it any less unbelievable.

Evangeline held up a finger, then took a much-need sip of her coffee. Bless Alex, she had doctored it just how she liked it—a bit of sugar and a whole lot of cream. Setting the cup on the table, Evangeline said, "Okay. Have at it."

Alex grinned so wide Evangeline thought her teeth would pop out and clop across the table like a set of wind-up chompers. "Okay, first, did you know we were witches before reading Dad's journal?"

Evangeline sat back, considering her answer. It wasn't the first question she'd anticipated, so she wanted to take a moment and choose her words. "Yes and no. I had started… awakening, as Carrow refers to it—"

"Carrow knows?" Alex asked, her brows high. "I'm shocked you told her."

"*She* told *me*." Evangeline pinched her mouth into a wry smile. "Carrow is a witch who can sense power in others. She knew what I was almost from the moment we met."

"Bitchin'."

Yeah, not so much. Evangeline cleared her throat. "I didn't have Dad's journal to clue me into what was happening. I honestly thought I was losing my mind."

"Why, what happened?" Alex rested her elbows on the table and leaned forward, adding in a quiet voice, "Did you see her, too?"

"Who?"

Alex settled in her chair. Shaking her head, she waved for Evangeline to continue. "Later. Go ahead."

Eyeing her sister, Evangeline debated continuing or pushing for more. Figuring they would get around to it, she let Alex's question drop. "I haven't seen anything. I *hear* things."

"Oh." Alex crossed her arms. "What sort of things?"

Evangeline bit her lip. It wasn't a secret per se, her

ability, at least, not to her family. But stating it like a normal everyday thing was kind of odd. Rather than do so, she said, "What happened to my red boots?"

Confusion flickered over Alex's face. "Huh?"

"My. Red. Boots," Evangeline stated.

Before moving to Whisper Grove, she had a pair of red leather ankle boots that she adored. As did Alex. And since they wore the same size shoe, Alex felt it her right to borrow the boots, despite Evangeline's firm and unequivocal no.

"Are you on those again?" Alex huffed. Taking a drink from her mug, she glared over the rim. "I already told you."

"Tell me again." Was it bad she enjoyed watching her sister squirm? At the time, Alex had sworn up and down she hadn't touched Evangeline's boots. They had, apparently, gone out for a night on the town and walked themselves through mud and muck before crawling to the very darkest corner of Evangeline's closet.

"I'm not the only one who wore them, you know? Mallory did, too."

The words were clear as a bell, not a hint of a whisper. Though she was telling the truth, her frown had turned mutinous, and it was obvious Alex didn't want to say more.

Evangeline pressed her lips together to keep from smiling. "On the night in question?"

"I didn't wear your stupid boots."

I wanted to look cute for my date with Bryan. I thought we were going to a concert, but the fool took me to a tractor pull.

Evangeline slammed her palm on the tabletop. "A tractor pull? You wore my boots to a *tractor pull*?"

Alex's eyes went wide. "Who told? I didn't say that."

"Oh, but you did." Smugly, Evangeline relaxed in her chair and regarded her sister. She couldn't stop her lips from curving, knowing Alex's fibs were a thing of the past. "My gift is to hear the truth." Or something... unspoken.

Alex blinked. Squinted. Frowned. Finally, she huffed a breath. "I'm going to have to move out."

Evangeline snorted. "You'll need a job for that." Ignoring Alex's eye roll, she rose and topped off her coffee. Moving toward her sister, she dug the anchor stone from her pocket and set it before her. It made a heavy clinking sound when Evangeline placed it on the wood.

"What's this?" Alex asked, picking up the stone.

"An anchor. Grace says it will help us focus to control and use our gifts." She watched Alex over the rim of her cup.

"This symbol is all over the house," Alex stated, lifting her gaze. "What does it mean?"

"Yeah, about that." Evangeline returned to her seat, proceeding to pour out the prior night's events for Alex. She told her of Carrow cloaking them so they could meet with the others, their family's history that brought them to Whisper Grove in the first place, and of the other witches in the coven.

"A coven? Like, an actual coven?" Alex's excitement rang in her voice. She slapped her hand on the table, her lips curving high. "Do I get a broom? What about a wand? I want in."

Evangeline massaged her temple. "It's not Hogwarts, Alex. Aside from Carrow, I don't know any of these people. Just because they need us doesn't mean we need them."

"What do you mean, need us?"

Evangeline rubbed her eyes, stalling. Knowing Alex, she'd rush right in because Evangeline told her not to. "It takes thirteen witches to complete a coven. They have nine."

"Four and nine is thirteen."

"Yes, your math skills astound me, Pythagoras."

"Stuff it." Alex pulled the ponytail holder off her wrist, yanked her hair back, and twisted it up. "Don't you get tired of being so…"

"Let me guess—boring?" Evangeline asked, tossing out Alex's favorite description of her.

"Controlled. When are you going to live, Evie?"

The soft words stung. Evangeline sucked in a harsh breath. Feeling suddenly defensive, she pushed up from the table, carried her cup to the sink, and dumped it out. "We can't all live carefree and adored."

The scrape of the chair sent a shiver down her spine as Alex joined her. Evangeline watched from the corner of her eye while Alex dumped her cup as well before leaning against the counter. "The point is to live a little. Just a little, that's all."

Evangeline lived plenty. Alex still saw her as an uptight, control freak. And while she still wore that hat occasionally, it wasn't the only one she owned. She could be fun. Even spontaneous. She just had to prepare for it first.

"So, tell me how this thing works." Alex held the anchor stone between her thumb and forefinger. "You gotta chant or rub it like a genie?"

Evangeline lifted the faucet lever. As she waited for the

water to run hot, she cut her eyes toward her little sis. "I have no idea how it works. Also, you rub the lamp, not the genie. Otherwise, you're looking at a whole different experience."

"I know, that's the point," Alex said, her brows bouncing up and down suggestively. Still leaning against the counter, she angled slightly away. "I've been seeing Mom."

Evangeline froze, then slowly pivoted toward her. "Where?"

"Here. Well, my room. When I look in the mirror Dad left us, I see her. Do you think that's my power—I can... see the dead?"

According to Carrow, one of Evangeline's sisters had that ability. Could a second? Did powers run through family lines, or did they pop up willy-nilly with no rhyme or reason? Probably something she should have asked last night when she was knee deep in a coven with her name on it.

Making a mental note to have Carrow size up Alex and Mallory, Evangeline said, "I honestly don't know. Use the anchor to focus. See what happens." God, she hoped that was good advice. She could see the hope brimming in Alex's eyes. What if it didn't work? And what if it did? Evangeline would either pee her pants or faint. When it came to spotting dead parents, there was no in between.

Bracing for either, she forced her shoulders up in a casual shrug. "Try it."

Alex shifted to the side with a nod, grasping the stone between her fingers. Her head bowed in concentration. Evangeline used that as an opportunity to dry the cups and put them back in the cabinets.

"Maybe if you say her name," she suggested, turning to her sister. "Oh my God!"

Her mother stood next to her. She was wearing the same pajamas Alex had been, holding the stone to her chest. She shot a foot into the air at Evangeline's yell. "What? Jesus H, what?" she shouted.

"Alex?" Gingerly reaching out, Evangeline touched her mother's hair. The curls were soft as silk between her fingertips. "Did you take your hair down?"

Her mom's mouth spoke, but it was Alex's voice. "No, it's still up. Why?"

Evangeline swallowed. Brushing her fingertips down her sister's forearm, she whispered, "You didn't conjure Mom. You *became* Mom."

Pounding echoed throughout the house. They both froze, and Evangeline wondered if she was sporting the same comically horrified expression as her mother. Alex. Brain jumbled, Evangeline shook her head at the strangeness of it.

Alex's hands flew to her face. "What do we do?" Then she was bouncing on the balls of her feet like a boxer. If she so much as took a swing, Evangeline would bash her in the head with a chair. After Alex removed Mom's face, of course.

More pounding, this time louder, was followed by, "Evangeline!"

"Shane?" she asked, moving toward the foyer. She frowned, trying to recall if they were supposed to meet up this morning. Behind her, Alex hissed, "What do I do? What if he sees me like this?" Panic laced her voice.

Evangeline spun to find her peeking out from the kitchen. "He's never seen Mom, so he wouldn't know, but drop the stone, you ding bat."

As if that reminded Alex she was holding the thing, she placed the anchor on the table. Before she'd fully pulled her hand away, she was Alex again. Evangeline blinked several times to make sure she had just witnessed reality, or if she was hallucinating. "That will never not be weird," she mumbled, continuing to the front door.

Before she could grasp the knob, it unlatched. The door slowly swung inward, revealing Shane with his arm lifted high to bang again. He stared at her a beat, then he was closing the distance between them.

"You're okay," he stated. Before she could wonder why he thought otherwise, he clasped both sides of her face and pulled her to his mouth for a kiss.

This was not a *hey, good to see you again* meeting of the lips. Not even an *I missed you* kiss. This was a kiss full of anger and promise, despair and hope. It curled her toes, leaving her breathless.

"Hot damn," Alex said from somewhere behind her. "I need to get me a mechanic."

Evangeline started laughing, and who the hell could kiss well when it was all teeth? Shane followed suit. Suddenly, they went from kissing to giggling. He pressed his forehead to hers. "I needed that," he said, sneaking a quick peck on her lips.

"The kiss or the laugh?" she asked, wrapping her arms around him. She loved being able to pull him close without reservation.

"Both." He sucked in a deep breath. It was then Evangeline noticed the tension in him. There was a definite tightness to his mouth, along with dark circles under his eyes.

Running her hand across his cheek, she frowned. "Are you all right?"

"I am now." He squeezed her reassuringly. "Can we talk a minute?"

"That's my cue. I'll go... stare at myself in the mirror." Alex's slippers made scuffing noises all the way up the stairs.

"You want some coffee?" Evangeline asked, guiding him toward the kitchen. As far as she was concerned, there was little a cuppa joe couldn't cure. Or least medicate.

"Actually, I can't stay. The shop opens in about half an hour, and I have a full schedule."

"Okay." She pulled out a seat at the table and sat. Worry simmered in her belly. Her man wasn't usually so grim and cryptic, so whatever had brought him to her door right after sunrise must be big. Her smile felt half-assed when she asked, "Are you breaking up with me?"

"What?" He laughed. Bringing her hand to his lips, he kissed her knuckles. "Not a chance. Why would you think that?"

Because you're being skittish. Duh.

Annnnd now she felt like an imbecile. Worse, a self-conscious imbecile. Men didn't usually kiss women like they were their reason for breathing, then dump them. And any who did needed a good, strong kick to their danglies.

"I'm an idiot on little sleep. Don't mind me," she weakly offered.

"Did you go out with Carrow last night?" he asked.

Surprise lifted her brows. "Yeah, did you see us?" As

soon as the words left her lips, she realized that was a moot question. The cloaking spell should have kept anyone from spotting them—but maybe he had because of his abilities? Perhaps he'd caught a glimpse of them streaking past at the speed of light in Carrow's attempt at stealth.

The whole night had been a jumble of revelations and more secrets, which added to her already-impressive confusion.

"Sort of." He shifted uncomfortably in his seat, clearly struggling with something. "I was *with* you."

"Huh. Fairly sure I'd have noticed."

"I don't get it either." He ran his fingers through his hair. "I experienced what you did last night. The car ride, the café, the creepy house. I was there, with you, until the basement. At least until *something* kicked me out."

She actually felt her brain skidding to a halt. All the saliva in her mouth dried up, and no matter how many times she replayed his words, they didn't quite compute. Yet, he'd ticked off all the places she'd gone last night. How would he know unless he'd been there?

Her lips curved into a knowing smile. "Did Carrow tell you that?"

His expression didn't lend itself to a joke. It was deadly

serious. "What time did you get home last night?"

"About two thirty."

"Right, so Carrow gave me a call at three to let me know she'd taken you to meet a bunch of strange women?"

Yeah, that probably hadn't happened. She shifted uncomfortably, trying to put the pieces together. "So... how did you find out?"

Shane leaned forward in his seat and opened his mouth, but a ringing cut him off. With a sigh, he reached into his back pocket and pulled out his cell. "Yeah?"

Buff's gruff timbre filled the line, but she couldn't understand what he was saying. Shane drew in a deep breath, exhaled a, "Be right there," and hung up the line, muttering, "Damn it."

Standing, he pushed his chair under the table, then bent and kissed her forehead. "I have to go. Apparently, no one knows how to drive anymore. This will be my third tow off Lune this week. Can we finish this tonight? Come over for dinner and... conversation." His brows danced suggestively.

She fluttered a hand at her heart, her best impression of a dignified, scandalized woman. "I love conversation. But I'm not eating that spaghetti again. How about I bring pizza?"

His laughter sent a shiver through her. It was a rich,

deep laugh she could listen to all day. "Probably for the best," he agreed.

She saw him to the door where he gave her another quick, unsatisfying kiss before leaving. Watching him hurry to his truck parked at the curb, she wondered how exactly he'd been able to be with her last night. While she loved a day off and usually wanted them to last forever, this one couldn't go fast enough—she was looking forward to the night.

Until then, she had witchy sisters to deal with.

Shane had just shut the bay doors for the night when the familiar choking growl of Evangeline's engine reached him. Shaking his head at the monstrous noise, he turned to lock the entrance with his key.

Walking out to meet her at the edge of the lot, he counted a full thirty seconds before the car came into view. She stopped next to him, then cranked the window down. "Hey, good lookin'. You need a ride?" It was followed by a flirty wink.

"I sure do." Shane leaned in through the window to brush his mouth over hers. Her lips smelled fruity, but tasted like lip balm. "Hmm, wax. My favorite."

Her nose crinkled. "Just for that, you can ride in back. The pizza already called shotgun."

Cocking his head to the side, he got a view of the three large boxes on the passenger seat. His eyes widened. "Do you think you got enough?" He was about to ask if he should expect some company.

Her head turned as she glanced at the stack. "One for each of us. Mushroom, pepperoni, and plain cheese. Fair warning—I've already called dibs on the mushroom. You and Buff can fight over who gets the other two."

Straightening, he peered at her. "You can eat a large pizza by yourself?" Was his skepticism showing? He could pull it off, but would regret it later. Where the hell did she put it—her hair?

"Probably beat ya done, too. Now get in before it gets cold."

Laughter rumbled from his chest. "God, I love you." He stole a quick kiss before climbing in behind the driver's seat. *Bad choice*, he realized with a grimace. With her long legs, the seat was back farther than he'd anticipated. He folded his legs in tight. By the time he was situated, his kneecaps could have been earrings.

His gaze caught hers in the rearview mirror. "Are you okay?" she asked, eyes crinkling with amusement. At his expense. "You look like you're in stirrups, ready to bear down and give birth."

"Oh, very funny," he grumbled. He tried to resituate himself. The attempt tweaked his back. "Just don't ever get me pregnant."

A snorting laugh broke free. Her hand flew to cover her mouth, but it was too little, too late. Her eyes narrowed on him in the rearview. "Stop making me do that."

"Darling, I have no control over it. On a totally unrelated note, remind me to get you a muzzle for Christmas," he teased, pleased when she lost the battle not to laugh. Twisted up like a pretzel in the back of a shuddering relic, uncomfortable as hell, Shane knew there was no place he'd rather be.

As soon as Evangeline put the car in park, Shane shoved his door open and unfolded from the backseat. "Remind me to never do that again. I call shotgun for infinity."

"Can't do that." Evangeline gathered her things—keys, phone, purse—and exited a hell of lot more smoothly than he had despite both hands being full. By the time she'd put everything in her bag, he'd walked around to the passenger side and picked up the pizza.

"Can you get the door? Buff came home an hour or so ago, so it should be unlocked."

She skipped ahead and cleared the way, and he carried the pizza into the kitchen, setting the boxes on the counter.

"I'm going to take a quick shower, then we'll see who the fastest pizza eater in Whisper Grove really is."

Evangeline straightened to her full height, staring him in the eye. "You're on, pretty boy."

Shane couldn't have held his smile if God himself had come down and slapped it off his face. He nearly said pizza be damned and carried her up to his room, but his stomach disagreed with that idea. And he smelled. A shower was definitely in order.

Taking the stairs two at a time, he hurried to his room, stripped on his way to his connecting bathroom, and stepped into the shower. Cranking the water on, he let out a yelp as the cold stream hit his skin. Not wanting to wait on it to heat, he grabbed the soap and started lathering.

As fun as he wanted their night to be, he needed to have a serious conversation with her about last night— about the things he'd seen and felt when he'd been with her. And how the hell *had* he managed to be with her, he still didn't know. Maybe she would have an idea. Or maybe it was part of her power or something.

He also wanted to get her take on the others he'd seen. He'd felt unwelcomed. Perhaps even threatened. And the snake-like figure winding through the women? Didn't like that at all. He'd seen it, but had Evangeline?

All he knew for sure was that he had no clue what had gone down in that basement, and though she'd come out of it no worse for wear, there were still too many doubts for him to brush off this heavy feeling in his gut.

Evangeline was an intriguing mix of strength and vulnerability. The last thing he wanted was to ask her to keep away from those like her, those who might be able to teach her how to come into her own, but then again, he didn't want her to blindly trust them either.

Shane dried and dressed as quickly as he'd showered, then headed down to the kitchen, ready to dive into dinner.

As he rounded the corner, he pulled up short. Buff and his girl were each hunched over an open pie box, slices stuffed into their mouths.

They stilled at his entrance. "You didn't wait for me?" he accused.

"Buff fed not hoo," Evangeline mumbled around a mouthful of dough. "Houf ruwes."

"House rules?" He glared at his uncle. "You tell her that?"

Buff pulled a deer-in-headlights. "Yef."

"Turds, the both of ya." Shane skirted past Evie, snatched the remaining box, and moved to the table. Pleased to see he'd been left with pepperoni, he pulled a slice free and took a bite, an appreciative groan tumbling from him

"I'm going to leave you young people to yourself and say good night." Buff stole a beer from the fridge, gathered up his box, then shuffled toward his room. "Thanks for the pizza, Winther. Next one is on me."

Once he was behind his closed door, Shane swallowed his bite. Leaning forward, he said, "Wow, you must be growing on him. He called you by name *and* offered to buy you dinner."

"My last name," she corrected.

"It's better than *that Winther girl*, like you brought the plague or something. Hell, he raised me, and I barely get that."

"He still calls you *that Winther girl*?"

"Yes," he deadpanned, earning him a snicker. Rising from the table, he headed to the fridge. "You want something to drink?"

"Water, please."

After snagging a bottle and a Coke for himself, he returned to the table, setting water beside her box. "Since we're being so honest, I was sort of hoping your sister would drop you off again. That way, I could talk you into spending the night."

Evie slowly lifted her gaze. Something in it made his pulse thud. "Bullshit. You just wanted to get your hands on Rosita. I saw your face when we rolled up in her. You can't deny it."

He grinned, popping the tab on his soda. Lifting it in toast, he said, "Guilty as charged. But just so we're clear—I'd like to get my hands on you both."

"Why, Mr. Carlson, I do believe I'm scandalized," she stated. Then she frowned, shoving the box across the table. She twisted the lid off her water bottle, taking a long swig before letting out a sigh. "I ate way too much."

Shane extended his neck to check her box. Four slices left. He let out a string of tsks. "That's weak, Winther. I thought you were going to eat me under the table."

Evie stretched, patting her stomach. "I concede. My eyes may have made lofty claims that my stomach couldn't live up to. I need pants with an elastic waist and a nap."

Not quite the evening he'd had in mind, but hey, whatever got her into his arms. Shane combined his leftover pizza with hers before flipping the lid and carrying it over to put in the fridge. After a hip-bumped the door shut, he said, "Come on, sleepy. Let's spread out on the couch."

She followed him into the living room. Taking a seat on

the middle cushion, he kicked his feet up onto the coffee table. When Evie joined him, snuggling in against his side, he wrapped his arm around her and pulled her as close as he could.

An appreciative purr left her as she draped one arm over his middle. "You're like my own personal furnace."

"You really do plan to fall asleep on me, don't you?"

"I stated as much, didn't I?"

More or less. And while he would love nothing better than for her to fall sleep in his arms, there was the still matter of her adventures with Carrow. He shifted his position to better see her. "We really need to talk, Evie."

Her warm sigh sank through his t-shirt. She pushed up and tilted to face him, curling one leg under the other. "Is this about last night?"

He nodded. "Want to tell me what happened?"

"Carrow took me to meet her coven. Man, it sounds bizarre to say that out loud." She shook her head. "I met—" she paused to tick off the number with her fingers "—five other witches. Actually, three other witches. Two were sparks."

"Sparks?"

"They're casters who have power, but they can't cast.

They add their power to the collective instead," she explained.

"Huh." He wondered which of the women he'd seen were the sparks and which were the witches. Not that he cared all that much, but it would be kind of cool to know what differentiated a spark from a normie if they couldn't do witchy things.

"It was kind of nice being around people like me. They were welcoming and friendly. I felt like I belonged. Grace—she's the elder—answered every question I could think to ask. Of course, I've had a million more since I left." Her mouth curved into a wry smile.

Shane covered her hand with his, giving it a gentle squeeze. "I'm glad you found them." He gave her hand a light pat. "But I got a different vibe from them."

Her brows drew together. "What do you mean?"

He exhaled a deep breath before answering. "I felt threatened. From the moment you took the first stair into the basement...it was as if something reared up its head and took notice. It was definitely *not* friendly or inviting."

Denial flashed across her features. "No, that can't be right. I mean, I was nervous walking down the stairs—who wouldn't be, especially after that hostage style ride to get there? You were probably just picking up on that. Speaking of which, how did you even tag along with me?"

A *pssht* escaped him. "Honey, I have no idea. I fell asleep, then I was with you. I *was* you."

"You what?" She focused on him.

His shoulders lifted. "I was experiencing everything from your point of view."

"That's bizarre. I've never heard of that. Not that I would have, but you know. I'll ask Carrow if she has."

His *hmm* came out before he could temper it. Her head jerked up, and he knew he had to phrase his concerns exactly right. "Given that we don't know it happened, I'd rather not tell anyone else yet."

She sucked her teeth. "You ask Buff?"

"Well, yeah..." He ran a hand down his face. "Buff is family. And he's like me. It would make sense that I ask him. Right?"

"Carrow is my friend. And she's like me. Wouldn't it make as much sense to ask her?"

Defeated in his argument, he slumped into the couch. "I walked right into that, didn't I?"

"More like tripped. But I sort of expected that answer, so..."

"You set me up." His lips pinched. He cocked a brow,

challenging her to deny it.

She scooted closer, pressing her body against his. An unfair tactic that gave her the advantage because her doing so made his eyes cross. How was he supposed to convince her of his side of the argument if his brain was on an amusement ride?

"But I do see your point," she whispered, fanning her warm breath against his ear. "Until we know more, I'll keep my mouth to myself."

He turned his head at that. Her lips were a hair's breadth from his. His heart trilled in his rib cage. "Are you seducing me to make me forget this conversation?"

"Is it working?"

He swallowed. "Yes."

She smiled in triumph. He pounced.

Chapter Seven

With a yawn, Evangeline pretty much dropped into the driver's seat. She waved to Shane, who was standing on the porch to make sure she got in safely. What kind of danger he thought she'd get into in his driveway, she didn't know, but he was vigilant.

They'd conked out somewhere around ten last night. As much as she loved falling asleep in his arms, her body did not like waking in them. She had a kink in her neck, a crimp in her back, and when she'd gotten up to use the restroom, she was limping like one leg was shorter than the other. On a scale of one to fifty on the comfort meter, she'd give him a six.

Besides, she was a creature of habit and preferred waking in familiar surroundings. Call her unromantic— Shane had—but with as many changes and upheavals as she'd lived in the last few months, the comfort of her own bed was one of the few consistencies she could count on.

Shane was cuddly and sexy as all hell, but he could not compete with her pillow. Also, the man was a cover hog.

She'd tossed and turned. He'd flipped, then flopped. Neither of them slept worth a damn. Though they hadn't broached the subject, Evangeline suspected Shane was still disgruntled from their conversation after dinner.

He thought the coven was a danger to her. She disagreed. The coven had not only offered her help, but also acceptance. They made her feel welcomed. They'd listened and answered questions she couldn't ask of anyone else. And the chance to learn her powers from people who were like her? Why would she turn her back on the opportunity? Because *Shane* had a bad feeling?

Maybe she *would* join them.

Maybe she *wouldn't*.

Maybe she'd introduce her sisters, if the time came. And maybe she wouldn't. But what she absolutely wouldn't do was cut off an avenue of possibilities based on fear. Especially when it wasn't her own.

The only thing they could agree on was keeping his strange ride-along a secret, even from Carrow. For now. And he wasn't entirely satisfied with that.

Evangeline hated they were grouchy with each other.

Ramming the key into the ignition with one hand, she buckled her seat belt with the other, getting caught up in the cross path. She let out a frustrated growl. This was why people shouldn't operate heavy machinery when tired. She could have easily strangled herself with the belt. Grumbling under her breath, she cranked the engine, then clicked the seat belt into place.

Lifting her gaze, she squinted against the glare of the porch light and blew Shane a kiss. He gave her a cocky wink that sent butterflies through her belly. Grouchy or not, that man was fine.

Another yawn later, she turned the wheel and gunned it, narrowly missing the porch in her U-turn.

His eyes rounded to the size of frisbees as her bumper skimped past. She offered an *oops* shrug that didn't appear to do much to calm him.

Ah, well. It was three in the morning. What did he expect at this hour? He ought to be grateful she'd thought to turn the wheel, or forget the porch—he'd be wearing the bumper.

Evangeline slowed at the end of his drive, glanced both

ways, then turned right. Between the hum—okay, more like grind—of her engine and the grittiness of her eyes, she was counting the minutes until her head could hit her pillow.

Dialing the radio to a rock station, she spun the volume almost all the way up. When the guitar riffs and yowling only added to the cacophony that she was zoning out to, she fumbled for the window handle and rolled it down.

Cold air blasted into the car, snatching her hair and whirling it into a frenzy. Shivering, she batted at the whipping strands. She couldn't see for shit, but hot damn, she was wide awake.

Slowing for the bend in the road, Evangeline noticed headlights in her rearview mirror, idly wondering what someone else was doing out at this ungodly hour. When she straightened out of the curve less than ten seconds later, the headlights were nearly on her tail.

The speed limit was not on this guy's agenda. Figuring he was in a hurry, she sped up so the driver had no reason to ride her ass.

Not only did the other car speed up as well, but he also flicked on his high beams.

"Shitass," she grumbled, scowling against the harsh lights reflecting off her mirrors. This time, she slowed to almost half the speed limit, waving out the window to let the other driver know it was safe to go around.

Even with the wind rushing through the window, the roar of the other engine filled her ears. At first, she thought it was to pass her.

Then her wheel jerked a hard left as the other car slammed into hers.

A terrified scream ripped from her chest. She clamped down on the wheel in a death grip. Eyes flying to the rearview mirror, she saw the headlights receding.

"Thank God," she muttered at the growing distance. She wanted to believe it was an accident—that the driver was turning tail and running away from his mistake. Except it hadn't been a mistake. There was no way the other driver hadn't seen her. And she'd made it as easy as possible to pass.

Evangeline stomped on the gas, causing her engine to whine in protest, but she kept her foot on the throttle until the speedometer was pushing eighty. Her car shuddered. She hunched forward, her grip on the wheel turning her knuckles shock white.

Only half a mile or so until she hit Main Street. Two to three blocks after that, she'd be in downtown, which gave her some measure of comfort.

If she could just reach town, she'd be safe.

She shoved a gaggle of curly strands out of her face,

knowing she would see a hell of a lot better if she could roll up her window. But the thought of taking even one hand off the wheel made her heart pound even harder.

Then a banging noise came from the engine. A beat later, the car started to slow, despite her mashing her foot on the gas. Her gaze dropped to the dashboard. The thermostat was nosing toward red.

"No, no, no," she chanted, peering into the rearview.

The headlights were inching closer again. Knowing it would do no good, she stomped the throttle. Her car was shaking almost as violently as she was.

All Evangeline could do was watch in horror as the other car zoomed in like a missile on its target. The impact jerked the wheel from her cold, cramping hands. Her car went into a skidding tailspin. Grappling for the spinning wheel, she tried to straighten it out before her car hit something unforgiving. The right-side tires slipped off the pavement, catching on the grass. Before she could comprehend what was happening, she was flipping through the air.

Shane was halfway up the staircase when his heart started racing. When he pressed his palm to his sternum, he was shocked at how hard it was pounding.

"What the hell?" Leaning against the wall, he took numerous deep breaths, relieved when his lungs worked as expected.

Seconds ticked past before his pulse slowed. Not to its normal pace, but enough he climbed the next step, then the next. Just when he decided the episode was over, a vice clamped around his heart, squeezing so hard he thought for sure he'd pass out.

Fear spiked throughout his body. His lungs, working fine a moment ago, locked up, refusing to process the air.

His spine shot straight. His vision narrowed to a dark, blurry tunnel.

He squeezed his eyes shut, willing the dizziness to pass, realizing too late that doing so sent his equilibrium ass over ears. He scrambled to grip the stair railing he couldn't see. Up was down, right was left, and he was screwed.

One knee buckled, and he rolled down the stairs like an out-of-control bowling ball.

The floor was gracious enough to catch him. When he finally came to a skidding halt across the carpet, his legs were straight up in the air. The last of his breath left his lungs on a groan.

Gingerly, he lowered his legs.

"What the hell was that noise?" Buff called, storming into the hall. He stumbled sideways to keep from stomping Shane's face. "Why are you playing dead on the floor?"

"I'm not playing, believe me," he mumbled, moving at the speed of a sloth as he forced himself to stand. Straightening his back slowly, he patted his body down. It wouldn't surprise him to find he'd broken something or his head was suddenly on backward.

"You okay?" Buff gripped his arm to steady him.

Shane gave his uncle a thumbs-up. "I think something happened to Evangeline." Then he lurched for the front door where he'd taken off his running shoes this morning.

"Jesus H, son, I can already see the stupid on you." Buff pushed past him, almost knocking Shane on his ass again, and bent to grab his shoes. Waving Shane to a kitchen chair, he shoved the shoes at him. "I'll drive."

Shane blinked, realizing Buff was right—he was in no condition to get behind the wheel. "Thank you."

"I can't have you killing someone, can I?" Buff grumped, shrugging into his coat. He yanked his keys off the hook by the door. "We're taking your truck."

Shane watched him thump out the door without a word, then shoved his feet into his shoes, not bothering with the laces. Grumpy Buff was Worried Buff, so Shane didn't take the bark personally. If he were in his uncle's shoes, he'd probably feel the same way.

Shuffling back to the staircase, he gingerly bent to grab his phone from the floor before leaving the house. Buff had the truck running and the heater on full blast when Shane climbed into the passenger seat. He glanced at his uncle, then his own lap. "Feels weird being on this side."

"Better than standing over some innocent schmo you ran off the road."

"Thank you, Captain Morbid." Shane turned the heat down to sweltering. "I wasn't complaining. I appreciate you driving." The last thing he wanted was to hurt someone. But he *needed* to get to Evangeline. His gut twisted into knots as he scanned the night.

He thought Buff mumbled *you're welcome*, but he could

have just as easily called him a jackass. Which in Buff speak was pretty much the same.

Buff turned toward town, and they rode in silence until the truck's lights glinted off the chrome bumper several feet past the ditch. If not for the bend in the road, he might not have spotted the robin's egg-blue of Evangeline's car.

Leaning forward in his seat, Shane pointed to the barely visible vehicle. "There. Pull over." His voice was calm, his breathing steady. But he was on the verge of a heart attack.

"Oh, hell," Buff muttered, shoving the gearshift into park.

Shane left his uncle to stare at the wreckage as he let gravity help him from the cab. His legs felt like warped two-by-fours on his trek across the field to the overturned car. He couldn't tell if his heart was racing too fast for him to notice, or if the organ had shriveled up in his chest, dead as a stone.

He was torn between wanting to rush forward... and running in the other direction. What would he find when he reached her?

Son of a bitch, he couldn't lose her.

Forcing his fear aside, he dropped to his knees next to the shattered driver's window. The pieces of glass glittered in the truck's headlights like confetti. Bracing his weight on his palms, Shane bent to peer inside. He hadn't realized he was holding his breath until it left his mouth on a whoosh.

Evangeline was hanging upside down, suspended by her seat belt. "Evie."

She didn't move.

Please let her be alive.

With trembling fingers, he checked her pulse. As soon as his cold fingers touched her skin, she jolted awake with a piercing scream that had everything from his eyebrows to his ass clenching tight.

He tumbled on said ass with a hollered, "Shit!"

"Shane?" she asked, blinking through her frown.

He started laughing. Then heard how unhinged it sounded and shut it down. Relief was a cool stream in his veins as he bowed low so she could see him. "Yeah, baby. It's me. Let's get you out of there."

A yank on the door handle confirmed it was stuck— either by bent metal or cold ground.

"Can you unbuckle and climb out the window?" he asked, sizing up the space to see if he could fit inside with her. Since he wasn't sure what her injuries were, he'd rather not, but as a last resort...

"No," Buff stated from behind him. "She'll land on her head. Plus, God only knows what kind of glass is in her hair. We'll push the damn car over."

"We?" Shane had the strength and dexterity of a baby giraffe. Rising to his feet, he tried to assume the position Buff told him to.

"Rock on one and two to get it moving, then all the way over on three. Got it?"

Shane nodded, and Buff counted them down. They rocked it on one and two, Shane still feeling unsteady, but then they put all their weight into the third push.

The car teeter-tottered, hung up in a weird, wobbly balance, then slammed down onto its tires.

Evangeline let out a yelp on impact.

This time when Shane yanked the handle, the door came free with a high screech of metal on metal. Having already unbuckled, she was struggling to get her legs around the seat.

"Here," he said, gently helping her out of the car. As soon as she was clear and on her feet, he wrapped her in his arms. She shivered against him. He hated to draw away from her, but he needed confirmation nothing was broken, bleeding, or ruptured.

Cupping her face in his palms, he peered into her eyes. "Are you hurt?"

Tiny pieces of glass fell from her hair when she shook her head. "I don't think so."

"You scared the hell out of me." He scanned her from head to toe, taking in the bloodied lip and black eye. Raising two fingers, he asked, "How many fingers am I holding up?"

"Thirteen," she said with a weak laugh. "Two, Shane. I'm fine. How did you know...?"

"The sorry sod rolled down the stairs like a kicked basketball. Thump, thump, thump," Buff told her. "Anything you want from the car?"

She frowned at his words. "My purse? My phone. I need to call Alex to come get me."

Buff shoved her retrieved bag into her hand. "No sense dragging your sister out. We'll take you home."

"And I'm staying. I'm not letting you out of my sight again," Shane declared, leaving no room for argument, agreement, or any other option. He couldn't take wondering if she was all right. This way, he'd make damn sure of it.

Thankfully, she nodded absently and allowed Shane to guide her to the truck. He watched her every step from the corner of his eye. For just emerging from a flipped car, she moved fairly well. She wouldn't take the dance stage any time soon, but he could at least guess that nothing was broken. Then again, she might have cracked a rib, knocked herself into a concussion, or even bruised an organ or two.

"What happened? You take the bend too fast?" he asked, more to keep her alert and talking than because he cared in that instant what had gone wrong with her junker. As long as she was okay, that was all that mattered.

Until she said, "No, someone ran me off the road."

He froze mid-step. "What?"

Even Buff, walking ahead of them, hitched to a stop to turn and stare at her. His gaze was tight with warning when it shifted to Shane. Then he stormed off ahead of them.

Shane gently swiveled her in his arms, making her look at him. He clenched his teeth to keep from saying, *Didn't I warn you?* He would remain calm and patient instead of bending her over his knee and spanking her pretty little ass. "You were run off the road?"

"Headlights appeared in my rearview mirror, a mile or so back. The next time I looked, they were charging up my tailpipe. At first, I sped up, thinking he'd back off. When I realized that wasn't working, I slowed and motioned for him to go around," she said, staring off into space.

Shane waited for more, his stomach churning at the glazed expression in her eyes. When she said nothing else, he snapped his fingers to get her attention. "And then what?"

She shrugged. "He hit me. Twice, actually. I lost control and..." She waved to the twisted metal mess behind them. "Can we go? I'm cold. I want to go home." She shivered, accentuating her point.

"Home?" After hearing what she'd been through, he had a different destination in mind. "You need to see a doctor. We're taking you to the hosp—"

The dazed girl in his arms turned into a hissing hellcat. She jerked out of his grasp. "No, I will not."

"Evie, honey, you rolled your car. You might have a concussion, or worse."

"I don't." She crossed her arms, bared her teeth, and, holy hell, the challenge in her narrowed gaze sent his gonads straight up with a twist to the left.

Disbelief lifted his brows. He ran a hand through his hair, regarding her in silence. Her chin tilted up in a move he recognized all too well. Stubborn, party of one. Blowing out a puff of air, he said, "I don't understand. Why don't you want to make sure you're all right?"

"Because I'm fine. I just lost my car, which means I'll have to buy a new one, so I can't afford a hospital bill."

"Who gives a shit about a bill?" he demanded, losing the leash on his temper. He threw his hands up. "I'll pay it. Do this for me. I'll take care of the bill."

"No." Mutiny was riding shotgun in her glare, with pride at the wheel. "I don't need you to pay my bills. I need you to take me home. If you can't, I'll walk."

"You'll walk," he repeated, because he couldn't believe the horseshit she was giving him. "I tell you what, my little witch, while you were tumbling bumper to bumper in that piece of shit car, I was tumbling, balls out and screaming, down a flight of stairs."

At her confused squint, he pushed in until the heat of her body warmed his and her eyes widened with uncertainty.

"When terror surged through your veins, it surged through mine. As the breath was stolen from your lungs, mine refused to breathe. When you koshed your pretty little head, my skull kissed the shit out of the floor."

There must have been something to his tone, or maybe it was the crazy he could feel settling over him, but Evangeline retreated until her spine was pressed flat against his truck.

"So, while you might be feeling fine and randy, I nearly broke my neck. And knowing you were scared and hurt nearly gave me a fucking stroke!"

His girl sucked in a gasp. "I'm sorry," she said, voice cracking with emotion an instant before she buried her face in her hands. "I had no idea."

Shane bit his tongue. He was still pissed, but he didn't need to be any more of a dick to make his point. "No, baby, I'm sorry."

Shame swamped him when she rushed into his arms, a crying, quivering mess. She let out a watery hiccup, and he added, "You can wipe the snot on my shirt."

"I already did."

Shaking his head, he gently turned her around and helped her into the truck, climbing in after her. The cab was warm thanks to Buff cranking the heat to full blast. Shane shot him a grateful look.

Buff glanced his way, lifted a brow. "Home?"

"Home," Shane parroted without inflection. Even if Buff dropped them at the hospital, Shane couldn't make her go inside and see a doctor. Well, he supposed he *could*, but it would result in one hell of a show for the hospital staff. He resigned himself to waking her every hour through the night.

Buff spun the dial on the radio, choosing a country station that made Shane want to curl into a ball and cry or shove spikes into his ears. At almost four in the morning, it was a toss-up.

"What about my car?" Evie asked in a small voice.

"Don't worry," Buff answered. "Once you're safely at home, I'll tow it back to the shop."

"Can you fix it?" she asked, hope brimming in her tone.

Shane's *pssht* beat Buff to the punch. "The frame is bent, and something was smoking when we left. It's not worth fixing, honey."

Her crestfallen expression almost made Shane offer to try, but really, the damn thing was a menace on wheels. Her money was better spent buying something more reliable. She would argue, but he'd help her find an affordable car that, at the very least, had airbags.

Shane scanned the road for another vehicle as they drove. He couldn't help the feeling that whoever had run her off the road was out there in the darkness, waiting for another chance.

He couldn't fathom why someone wanted to hurt her, but his gut told him she was in more danger than he'd originally realized. Shane would do whatever it took to keep her safe—even if that meant he had to hog-tie her to his side.

Chapter Eight

"If you wake me one more time, I'm going to choke you with your own tongue."

Shane had kept his promise to wake her every hour on the hour, shining a mother-loving flashlight into her eyes each time. If she weren't concussed from the wreck, she would be from his nursemaid routine. After the third seizure-inducing retinal check, she'd tried to swipe the light and give him a colonoscopy he'd never forget.

Unfortunately, his agility outmatched hers and he escaped unscathed. But she wasn't done with him—a sneak attack was in the making. Far off in the making because, for the love of God, all she wanted was to sleep.

"Last time, I promise." The light clicked off, returning the room to darkness. Sweet, blessed darkness. "I have to go drop off this week's deposits at the bank before the shop opens."

"Deposits? Don't most people pay by credit card?" she mumbled, tucking the blanket under her chin. Why did her eyes feel as though her lids had been taped open in a sandstorm? Oh, right, because her boyfriend had highjacked her rest.

"Eh, more and more, but we have a sturdy group of older customers who prefer check or cash. They don't believe in spending on credit. Apparently, debit confounds them. Or it's a tool of the devil or something."

"Those cagey geriatrics..." Her eyes drifted shut.

"Did you just fall asleep on me?" Shane asked, tucking a strand of curls behind her ear.

"Yes. Now get out so I can keep at it." She flopped her hand to shoo him along. "I need a few hours before work."

He said nothing for so long she was nearly out cold when he asked, "Given what you just went through, do you think that's a good idea?"

"What, going into work?" She reluctantly pried one eye open. "No, but I just got back after being off for weeks. I wouldn't put it past Mimi to write me up."

"For wrecking your car?" Skepticism coated each word.

"Have you met my boss? She'd write me up if I had died. Besides, I have to buy a new car now, so it's either work more hours or prostitute myself on the corner. Your pick."

He shook his head. "I don't like it."

"More work or prostituting myself?" she asked with a lazy grin.

He didn't match it. In fact, he wasn't sporting much humor at all. His gaze held. He crossed his arms. Rolling onto her back, she stretched with a groan. She really was too tired for this conversation.

"I think you should take the day to rest," he stated. When she opened her mouth to protest, he added, "Barring that, at least take it easy and call me as soon as you get home. I'll stop by after I close the shop."

"Okay. Get out so I can miss you," she mumbled.

"My heart pitter-patters at your sweet words." Shane pressed a kiss to her temple, then adjusted her covers, tucking her in all nice and snug. "I'll see you tonight. Love you."

"Me too," echoed from her lips as she slipped into dreamland.

An appreciative groan escaped as Evangeline finally hobbled off the last step. Her calves were cramping as if she'd run a marathon—in high heels. On gravel. She could barely turn her head because her neck was so stiff, and some sneaky asshole had twisted her spine into a knot while she slept.

That's what you get for flipping your car.

She slumped against the railing. Ugh, her poor car. As if losing her only means of transportation weren't bad enough, she had to wake up feeling like a post-autopsy corpse as well?

Releasing her grip on the banister, Evangeline carefully shuffled to the kitchen. Shane was right—she needed to rest today. The thought of hauling books all over the library made her want to curl up in a corner and cry. Unfortunately, she was also right in that she couldn't afford to skip a day of work.

Making it through her shift on no sleep would require a miracle of caffeinated proportions.

Speaking of which, she needed coffee, STAT. Too many thoughts were darting around her exhausted mind.

After last night, she couldn't deny someone had intentionally attacked her. However, acknowledging it and accepting it were two different things. She needed time to process everything that had happened—from meeting the coven, to Shane's insistence something wasn't right, to the wreck.

Even after Shane had cleaned her scrapes, given her numerous flashlight eye exams, and finally tucked her into bed, she hadn't been able to believe someone wanted to hurt her, that the wreck had been intentional. There was still a desperate part of her clinging to it being an accident.

Because why would anyone want to run her off the road? To scare her? Possibly. But why? What was the point?

To kill her?

A shiver snaked down her spine. Whoever had rammed her car had to have realized she could have died—yet, they'd done it anyway.

The clank of dishes sounded from the kitchen, reminding Evangeline that she had braved the staircase for her much-needed java fix. Pushing through the swinging door, she found Alex putting away dishes from the dishwasher. She even dried them with a towel first.

Evangeline paused to stare. "Have I entered an alternate reality?"

Alex peered at her over the rim of a plate. "Nervous

energy. I have a job interview this morning."

"Oh. Oh, that's *great*." Evangeline leaned on a kitchen chair for support. Her back was killing her.

Alex loved idle time, but thrived when busy. A job was just what she needed to plant roots here and make friends. Lazing away in the house wasn't good for her.

"Where?"

"The café." Alex shrugged, placing the plate in the cupboard. "It's not anything to dance a jig over, but I need to get out of this house, and since I can't go on a shopping spree ..." She gave Evangeline a knowing smile.

Evangeline returned it. Until her gaze snagged on the empty coffeepot. Her heart pulled a tumbleweed routine in her chest. Pointing to the pot, she demanded, "Why is that empty?"

"I couldn't get it working," Alex answered with a nonchalant lift of her shoulders. "I don't know what's wrong with it."

"Is it plugged in?" Evangeline squeaked, eyes narrowing on the outlet. The cord was plugged in. Dear God, the universe really was trying to snuff her.

"I've unplugged and plugged it in twice, shook it, slapped it, talked crap to it. I even cooed and sang it a lullaby. Nothing. But I knew you would appreciate my efforts."

"I'd appreciate them more if you'd gotten the piece of shit working," she said, sinking into the chair. Of all the mornings... Rubbing her fingertips against her temples, she asked "What time is your interview?"

"Eleven." Alex turned, wiping her hands on a dish towel. "Why?"

Evangeline moaned her misery. "I have to be at work by ten. Do you know how many children come through those godforsaken doors? I cannot live like this."

Alex soft laughter made her scowl. "Stop at the café before you go into work. It's on the way, right?"

"Yeah, but..." Evangeline bit her lip. "I don't have a car."

It took a moment for her words to sink in. Alex's brows drew together. "What?"

"I wrecked last night on the way home from Shane's. My car is totaled."

Alex's mouth dropped open. "Is that why you're walking like you rode a camel from here to Egypt? When I saw Shane leave this morning, I just assumed..." Her brows danced over her forehead.

"That he beat me in my sleep?" she asked. Given his overzealous use of his flashlight, she felt the statement wasn't too far off.

"Whatever floats your boat. How are you going to get to work?" As soon as the question left her mouth, Alex stiffened. Her pale eyes hardened. "Don't even ask."

No dummy, her sister. Evangeline flapped her hands in the air. "I barely made it down the stairs for coffee—which you failed to provide—how am I going to make it several blocks to the library?"

"On your hands and knees," Alex suggested on a growl. "I'd rather set my bikini line on fire than give you Rosita."

"Hey, at least I *asked*," Evangeline tossed back. Sleep deprivation and the horror of the night before converged to bring out her snark. Never a good way to ask for a favor. "You would have just snatched the keys, then played dumb when caught."

Alex's eyes rolled so hard Evangeline half expected a grinding sound to accompany the movement. "You are *not* equating Rosita to boots. I can buy you another pair of boots. You couldn't afford a single part on Rosita."

Alex had no idea how right she was. Still, Evangeline was so not in the mood to walk. Frustration bared her teeth. "It's a few blocks, Alex. The speed limit is thirty-five. Do you really think I'd let anything befall her? I know your temper too well. Besides, it's supposed to rain later. I really don't need pneumonia on top of everything else."

Perhaps that was stretching the sympathy line a bit thin, but hey, she had to dig deep because Alex had the emotional range of a toothpick.

Her sister honored her with a glare.

Evangeline forced her aching body to stand. "Never mind."

"You owe me," Alex blurted, lacing her arms under her chest. "If anything, and I mean *anything*, happens to my car, I will have you cremated and put in Chester's litter box."

"You are too kind." Truth be told, Alex could have knocked Evangeline over with a snort. She had hoped her sister might offer to drop her off, but figured she'd be hoofing it to work. Never in this lifetime had she thought Alex would agree. It left her off kilter. "What about your job interview?"

"I'll walk in your black combats. They'll look great with my mini skirt."

"Deal." Evangeline offered her hand.

Ignoring it, Alex stated, "This is a one-time thing, and only because you're moving around like George Burns. Buy a new car." She spun on her heel, then marched from the kitchen.

Evangeline watched the swinging door swish back and forth. A new car, right. She'd have the money for that in, oh, seven years. Until then, she'd get a lot exercise in because she knew from experience Alex wouldn't budge on this favor being a one-time thing.

But today, she'd drive a badass boss bitch of a car. Smiling, Evangeline returned to her room to get ready for work.

The Mustang's engine rumbled as Evangeline pulled up to the curb in front of The Brew, the steering wheel vibrating softly beneath her fingertips. Rosita had a hell of a lot more power than she was used to. Certainly more than her poor hot mess of a car. *May she rest in peace.*

Evangeline slid the gear shift into park, peering through the café's large front window. Though the early morning rush had passed, every table was full, and she counted half-a-dozen people waiting in line. The urge to drive on by pressed on her shoulders, but she really didn't want to spend the next five hours in a caffeine-deprived state. Especially since her shift was scheduled with Mimi.

No coffee plus Mimi had *fired* written all over it.

She turned off the car and pocketed the keys, gambling the line would move fast enough to get her to work on time. If not, well, at least she'd have coffee to sip while her boss raised holy hell.

Hurrying through the door, she took her place in line and scanned the menu board over the counter. She didn't usually buy coffee and breakfast, mostly because it was money better spent elsewhere, so she wasn't sure what to order. The options were overwhelming.

Soon, she was next in line. The girl behind the counter disappeared to fill the order of the previous customer, giving her an extra minute to decide between a blueberry muffin or a banana nut.

"Holden, would you mind getting the next customer before you go?" the girl asked.

The young man from the night Carrow introduced her to the coven moved to the register. "What can I get you?"

Her brain sputtered. Hadn't the name Holden been mentioned at the 'meeting'? Was he part of the coven? Did he recognize her, too?

Yes, I recognize you. Please place your order.

Her mouth went slack. Her eyebrows shot high. Luckily for her, she couldn't see how stupid she looked. But she felt it.

Stop being so obvious. Order something.

"Hot caramel latte and a blueberry muffin," she blurted.

"Size?"

"Uh, small."

Holden punched in her order. "Whipped cream?"

She nodded.

"Six twenty-three."

After Evangeline dug a ten out of her bag, she handed it over. He passed her the change, then motioned her to move aside to wait on her order.

Questions darted through her skull. She was dying to know if reading her mind was his gift or a spell. Drumming her fingers on the countertop, she waited anxiously for him to return.

He didn't. The girl set her coffee and a bag on the counter. "Here you go."

"Thanks," Evangeline murmured, trying to catch another glimpse of him. The kid had probably read her intentions and ran off. Feeling let down, she gathered her stuff and turned to leave. And plowed right into someone.

The lid popped off the cup, sloshing hot coffee over her hand and the other person. Jumping back, she dropped her cup and the bag with her muffin, and the rest of the scalding, frothy liquid spilling over the floor.

"Oh my God, I'm so sorry," she said, lifting her eyes to the person she'd run into.

Freya Stone stared back at her with a cold, hard gaze.

Of course it would have to be Freya. And *of course* the woman was decked out in an expensive-looking white coat and matching gloves. Or she had been. Evangeline's coffee had added brown splotches along the front.

If there had been any doubt—there hadn't—Evangeline was now certain the universe wanted her dead. She swallowed whichever organ it was that had climbed her throat. "Freya, I'm so sorry. I didn't see you."

Rather than accept her apology—or punch her, which, given the woman's expression, Evangeline kind of expected—Freya slowly brushed her gloved hand over the stained fabric of her coat.

Dear God, was that angora? Sweet baby Jesus, if you love me even a little, let it be fake.

"Clearly," Freya said quietly, but with enough venom to drop a horse.

The entire shop had gone silent. Evangeline could feel

the collective gaze pressing down on her. Probably waiting on a cat fight to break out, the scum suckers.

Evangeline spun back to the counter. She grabbed a fistful of napkins in each hand, and then attempted to clean up the mess she'd made. Patting the front of Freya's coat, Evangeline again offered a sincere apology. "I don't know what to say, Freya. I really am so very sorry."

Freya just stood there, glaring holes in Evangeline's skull, as she lamely tried to soak up the liquid from the soft fabric.

Was it just her, or were things getting more awkward by the minute? Most of the patrons had gone back to their own business, but she felt as if a spotlight was shining directly on them. Sweat slid down her spine. Her belly dropped to the floor.

Giving up, she let her hands flop to her sides. "Can I pay for your order?"

Freya's gracious response was a level, "You really are a plague on this town. All of you Winthers. Always have been, always will be."

What could Evangeline say to that? *Thanks? You're wrong? Up yours?*

"I'm sorry, but flattery won't work." With that, the contrition she'd felt moments ago vanished. The bitch didn't want her apology? Fine. It'd be a cold day in hell's pantry before she offered another.

If Evangeline had a pair, she'd grip Freya by the back of her perfectly coifed blonde head and introduce her pearly, even teeth to the counter at a high rate of speed. Evangeline's mother would cluck at such nastiness, but hey, Mama had never met the likes of Freya Stone.

Was it too much to ask God to smite the snooty bitch, right here, right now, so Evangeline could witness it? She sent up a prayer for that very request, or at the very least, for God to give the woman a voracious, untreatable case of crabs.

Today was not the day to mess with Evangeline Winther.

"What is it about me that gets your goat?" she asked, genuinely curious. From the moment they'd met, Freya had hated her guts. "Is it that I'm smarter than you? Or is it because I have Shane?"

Freya's icy smile rolled over her. "Maybe I just don't like you. Surely I'm not the first in your life who doesn't."

You wouldn't understand, perfect little Winther.

The sentence whispered beneath Freya's words, and Evangeline nearly snorted at *perfect.* It certainly wasn't the "truth" she'd expected to hear from the ice queen.

Asking for clarification bubbled on the tip of her tongue, but she didn't want Freya to know she'd heard.

"As much as I'd like to exchange more insults, or, better yet, shove you into a port-a-potty and kick it downhill, I've got more important things to do." Evangeline used the napkins that had done nothing for Freya's coat to wipe up the puddle on the floor before tossing them, her empty cup, and her soggy muffin into the trash. "How about you stay out of my way, and I'll stay out of yours? Have a great day," she said, letting her smile tack on *bitch*.

Then she gathered what little dignity she had left and walked out the door.

Evangeline's legs carried her to the Mustang, but as soon as the door was open, they dumped her on the front seat. Her hands were shaking as she pulled the key from her pocket and forced it into the ignition.

Whether it was the confrontation with Freya, the rough night, or the disappointing lack of coffee, she couldn't stop the tremors. She decided to blame the cool morning air and leave it at that.

She cranked the key, and the Mustang roared to life. Grinning at the rumbling power under her control, she glanced at the coffee shop. Freya stood at the large window, arms crossed, scowling at her.

Evangeline had the inexplicable urge to wave, earning

her an even more fervent death glare from her nemesis. She'd take what she could get. Throwing the car into gear, she turned the wheel and floored it.

Chapter Nine

"Thank you, Mr. Carlson. Have a great day."

"Thanks. You, too, Debbie." Shane grabbed the cylinder to retrieve his deposit receipt. As much as he liked money, he had an odd aversion to depositing it. Once a week, he forced himself to the bank if he couldn't talk Buff into going for him.

After leaving Evangeline's house, he'd swung by home for a quick shower, hit the garage for the money bag, and headed to the bank.

He was driving away from the teller window when he spotted Rosita parked in front of The Brew. His gaze slid over the sleek lines of the Mustang. He started to turn left out of the parking lot when a familiar bounce of curls snagged his attention.

Evangeline darted out of the coffee shop. She scrambled around the hood, then all but dove into the front seat, slamming the door behind her. Irritation soared at seeing her behind the wheel. She was in no condition to drive any car, much less one with that much power. What bargain had his girl made with her sister to get the keys to Rosita?

The bank was a block catty-corner from the coffee shop, but he heard the engine roar to life an instant before Evangeline sped away. Evie driving Rosita left him dazed, but the bigger shock was when Freya stepped from the coffee shop to watch the Mustang leave.

And she was lit up like New York on New Year's Eve. A rusty orange color swirled around her head, growing murkier with each passing second, and Shane realized all the ill-will surrounding her was directed at Evangeline.

"Fuck my duck," he croaked, eyes glued to his glowing ex-girlfriend. Freya Stone was a witch.

He couldn't have been more shocked if he'd woken up with his nipples hooked to a car battery.

Freya marched to a shiny silver Audi parked several yards behind where the Mustang had been. There was no roar of her engine when she started the car, but a beat later, she, too, sped off in the same direction as Evie.

Rather than turn left to his garage, he rotated the wheel right and gunned it with a shriek of his tires, cutting off another car as he shot down the road. Keeping his distance, Shane trailed Freya.

Her Audi slowed at the library—looking for Evangeline? Shane glanced over the front lot but didn't see the Mustang. Maybe she'd come to her senses and called in. Then again, work was about the only reason he could think of that would convince Alex to let Evie tool around in Rosita.

Figuring his girl had simply parked behind the library, he glanced at the dashboard clock. He was cutting it close if he wanted to get back to the garage before Buff opened the bays. Starting the day behind meant he'd be later than he wanted tonight to check on Evangeline.

Just as he decided another five minutes was his limit, Freya cut a hard right down Wellington, darting through the steel gates of Stone Manor. Shane slowed to a creep, peering through the slats to watch Freya.

Stone Manor was as uppity as it sounded. Built over a hundred years before the Stone family moved in and gave it the pompous moniker, it was the largest home in Whisper Grove. Even the Winther house couldn't compete with this stone monstrosity.

In high school when he and Freya had been an item, Shane had avoided the place. A home should be warm and inviting. Stone Manor was the opposite, reminding him of a morgue—all business, just waiting on the dead people to arrive.

He shuddered at the chilly memories.

Freya climbed from her car, slamming the door. "What the hell were you thinking?"

Who was she talking to? Sinking low in his seat, Shane rolled down the window to listen. He had no idea what he'd do if she spotted him.

Freya stomped around the front of a black sedan, her stare pausing on the hood. Her face pinched into a snarl. She lifted a phone to her ear, and Shane realized she must have been screaming into the cell before. What he wouldn't give to hear the other end of the conversation.

"Why would you do that?" she shouted, spinning toward the house. "I told you I had it covered."

Once she disappeared behind the heavy wooden door, Shane crept forward until he could peek through the gate for a better look at the black car.

His blood froze.

Long scrapes of the ugliest robin's egg-blue highlighted the buckled dent in the hood.

It was the car that had smashed into Evie.

Witchful Thinking

As if waking stiff and pissy, then dumping her coffee on Freya Stone and her breakfast on the floor wasn't rough enough, Evangeline now had to face her boss without the necessary armor.

With a cup of joe, she could face almost anything. Without it? She shivered.

Not wanting to tempt fate, she tried to sneak in the back door of the library with her key. Naturally, that plan followed the theme of the day—of the whole stinking month—and refused to cooperate.

"Piss and moan," she grumbled, trying to force the key to turn. It took three tries of inserting and removing said key before the lock clicked to the left. By then, she was ready to bash the glass with a rock.

Not a good tactic for stealth.

The longer she avoided her boss, the better. Maybe she'd get lucky and Mimi would be home sick with the black death. That bubble of hope burst when she rounded the corner into the office and nearly made out with the woman in question. And her steaming, filled-to-the-brim mug of tea.

Evangeline veered to the left with a yelped, "Sorry," continuing to the table on the far side of the room. Pulling out a chair, she dropped her purse into it and pivoted to find Mimi's expression close to a smile.

"Ooh, that would have burnt us both," the evil woman said, blowing into the cup.

Evangeline scanned the room. Was Mimi speaking to her, without rancor? Where was the pithy comment about her clumsiness? Or the threat to fire her because her hair was too curly? Scathing conversations like those were so much a weekly event that Evangeline came in locked and loaded with scathing retorts.

How could she make snide remarks about her choice in clothing or her pompadour if Mimi didn't insult her first? That she hadn't insulted her was insulting.

Taking in the woman's sedate gray slacks and black blouse, Evangeline almost asked, "Who are you and what have you done with my boss?" but did she really want to know? If someone had taken her, they could keep her, bless their hearts. No returns accepted.

"You look nice," she said instead, meaning it. The neutral palette was a much better match to her skin tone and hair color than her usual wear. Not to mention Evangeline's retinas—one could only take so many hibiscus flowers on neon fabric before their eyes permanently crossed.

"Celia is supposed to be in today," Mimi said by way of explanation before blowing a long breath over her tea. Steam rose from the cup, making Evangeline all the more grateful she hadn't done to Mimi what she had done to Freya.

That was as far as her good news went, though. Celia was Mimi's boss, and she boasted the fun-loving, vivacious personality of a Cape Buffalo. Only with a touch of drill sergeant added in for kicks. The woman made militant Mimi seem like a carefree hippy in comparison.

"I'm so delighted to hear that," Evangeline rolled out dryly, typing in her credentials at the log-in screen. Crap rolled downhill when Celia was in town—not because Celia barked orders, but because Mimi did. If Evangeline had known Celia would be in, she would have tossed money cares to the wind and called out with an enlarged prostate or something. Anything to avoid Mimi's uptight, stressed wrath.

Except she seemed relaxed this morning, didn't she? Evangeline narrowed her eyes on the other woman. What sort of trickery was she up to? As if sensing her unease, Mimi smiled and left the office.

Definitely up to trickery.

Evangeline finished clocking in, and then texted Carrow.

After last night, she realized she needed to protect Shane as much as he needed to protect her.

Can you stop by the house this afternoon? I get off at three PM.

She set her phone on the table before shoving her purse into her filing cabinet drawer. It wasn't the most secure place to store things, but it was better than leaving her stuff out in the open. Still, every time she did it, she wished the cabinet had a lock. Her phone chimed.

Sure. What's up?

I want you to show me how to create a protection spell. Can you do that?

Witch, please. I'll be there with tassels on.

Evangeline squinted at her screen. Tassels? WTF kind of protection did Carrow have in mind?

Figuring she was better off not knowing, Evangeline dropped her phone into her purse and shut the file cabinet. As long as whoever had tried to hurt her couldn't do the same to Shane, she didn't care what kind of spell she used, tassels or no.

Leaving the office, she went in search of Mimi to ask what morbid tasks she had planned for her. For some reason, Mimi got off on her misery. Hands on her hips, Evangeline scanned the lower floor for her boss.

The temperature suddenly dropped several degrees, enough to send a shiver through her. Evangeline craned her head around to see who had opened the door.

The doors were closed. No one was in the lobby. Frowning, she glanced to the clock behind the counter. The library didn't officially open for another ten minutes.

"That was weird," she muttered, heading for the stairs.

But Mimi wasn't on the second floor either. Evangeline leaned over the short balcony, glancing from the main glass doors below to the check-out counter. Unless she'd missed Mimi on her sweep of the first floor, she had to be in the bathroom... or the basement.

Evangeline jerked back. She would rather walk in on Mimi as she danced naked to the *Thong Song* than go anywhere near that basement. There was nothing in this world that could get her down those stairs again. If Mimi had gone down, she was on her own.

Did that make her a chicken?

Cluck, cluck.

Rubbing a palm down her face, Evangeline decided to shelve the books on the return cart. Busy, mindless tasks would work wonders for her tired state anyway.

Besides, shelving the books would force her to bend and stretch, and the more she used her muscles, the better they would feel. The stiffness she'd woken with was already fading. Now, all she needed was a caffeine drip to make it through the day.

Her mind flashed to the boxes of tea Mimi kept stocked in the break room. Any other day, she'd rather go without caffeine than to consider tea, but desperate times and all that.

When she stepped off the bottom stair, a rush of cold air enveloped her. "What the hell?" Rubbing her arms, she pivoted to the doors again.

Winther...

Evangeline froze, not entirely sure she'd heard what she didn't want to. When nothing else sounded, she forced a breath from her lungs. She was tired, beaten up, and lacking her go-go juice, so it was a fair bet her imagination was wonky right now. There was no reason to believe she'd heard a thing as she wasn't even near the basement. Right?

Help us...

Okay, not her imagination. But also, not her responsibility, either. Hearing them did not make them her problem.

She'll come after you, too...

A deflating balloon sound left Evangeline's lips as she retreated toward the office. "Piss on you and this place," she declared to the empty room. "I'm not doing shit."

"Excuse me?"

The unexpected voice—outside of her head—sent her liver into her chest. Evangeline tilt-a-whirled with a scream, coming face to stoic face with Celia. The hard look in the other woman's eyes suggested she'd overheard her.

"Celia, hi," Evangeline said, "I was, uhm, rehearsing my lines." Her smile felt too wide, too clownish, and yet, she couldn't unhinge her jaw long enough to straighten the grin. Why couldn't her power have been teleportation? She'd have learned that shit in a minute.

Celia didn't respond at first, just gave her a bland onceover. "Where is Melissa?"

Who's Melissa? was on the tip of Evangeline's tongue, but she bit it back. Why Celia insisted on the formality of her full name when Mimi did not was beyond her.

"She's not here." Evangeline scowled at the mistake. "No, I mean, she's *here*, just not *here*."

Jesus, if ever a bolt of lightning is to strike me, now seems the appropriate time.

Evangeline pointed to the office. "I'll go see," she offered, already halfway across the floor. By the time she skirted around the counter, Mimi was exiting the hallway.

"Evangeline—" Mimi started with a tone she knew all too well.

"Celia's here!" Evangeline waggled her hand toward the other woman. "Looking for you."

Mimi changed course. Counting on a few minutes of privacy, Evangeline all but raced to the bathroom. Putting her weight against the door, she forced it shut and stood there until her pulse slowed.

Finally, she shuffled to the sink and twisted the cold knob. She splashed water on her face. Then again. Her reflection was glassy-eyed and pale, leaving her freckles to stand out against her skin. The dark circles under her eyes completed the recently risen-from-the-dead-look.

Evangeline twisted the water off, then shook the droplets from her hands. She reached for a towel from the dispenser on the wall.

Winther...

The whispers had always filled her with fear, from the moment she'd first heard them to a few minutes ago in the lobby. Her pulse raced, and her mouth went dry. But this time, something else surged through her veins. It was scorching hot and freezing at the same time. It sat, coiled and heavy, on her chest, waiting for her to let it out.

Lost...

Evangeline lifted her gaze to the mirror. Although she appeared the same as moments before, there was something different in her.

It was as if a veil had parted, and all that had been hidden deep inside was rising to the surface. This energy that blazed through her body was her power— be it a gift or a curse. It was *hers.*

Trapped...

Claiming control over it instead of the other way around was freeing. Slowly, she turned from the mirror, quieted her mind, and listened. Not to the voices, but to the energy sizzling through her veins.

The dark—

"*Silence.*" The command rolled from her with a low wave of energy. One word, but so powerful. Evangeline let out a surprised laugh as the quiet echoed off the bathroom tiles.

Straightening, she surveyed the room. "I'm willing to listen, but not like this. I have my own life, with my own problems, and all you're doing is making everything harder. If you want my help, it will be on my terms. Not yours."

When the only sound was the drip of the faucet, she added. "I promise I will come to you when I'm at a point where I can help. Deal?"

Several voices rose together to answer. *Yes.*

For the first time in weeks, control and peace returned to her. Evangeline gave the mirror one satisfied smile, then left the bathroom and her fears behind.

Chapter Ten

"Hello?" Shane called, peering into the empty foyer. He waited, but all he heard was music coming from somewhere upstairs. Another shouted *hello* earned a soft meow as Chester sauntered in from the kitchen.

The house had let him in, but he hesitated to enter without one of the girls knowing. At the same time, he didn't want to stand in the entryway until one of them noticed, either.

He walked to Chester, bent and gave the cat a scratch behind the ears. "You know where I can find my girl?"

Chester turned his dark head to peer at the staircase. His cut-off meow sounded like "Up." Straightening, Shane studied the cat with a frown. Either his marbles were rolling free, or Chester understood him.

"Marbles are definitely on the loose," he dismissed with a chuckle and climbed the stairs. Especially after what he'd learned about Freya. He couldn't say for sure if Freya was responsible for Evie's wreck, but he definitely wanted to warn his girl to stay away from her.

Music filtered through Evangeline's closed bedroom door. He knocked, glancing around the balcony to the other shut doors. He wondered if her sisters were out and about or tucked in their bedrooms.

Knocking again, he twisted the knob. He poked his head through the cracked door. The blow dryer kicked on, cutting off his "Evie?"

Shane entered her bedroom, then followed the noise to the bathroom where he stopped cold. All thoughts of Freya fled his mind at the sight before him.

Evie, his lovely, brilliant librarian, was gyrating across the tile floor to *Livin' La Vida Loca*. Her head whipped back and forth, curls propelled by the hot air flying everywhere, as she sang along to the lyrics.

Enjoying the view, Shane canted against the counter and let his gaze roam. The faded T-shirt bunched and twisted with her movements, each shimmy and shake giving him glimpses of her striped pink panties. He slid his palm across his jaw and over his mouth in an attempt to mute his laughter.

Evangeline froze, dryer blowing one side of her hair

back from her head. She haltingly turned, and even though he saw it coming, her scream shriveled things on him better left unshriveled.

"You scared me," she accused, switching off the dryer. Shaking it in the air, she added, "Don't sneak up on me."

"I knocked and called your name," he explained with a lift of his shoulder. As she stood eyeing him from under wild hair, she looked like a human incarnation of static electricity. He rolled his lips between his teeth, but his grin was getting harder to suppress than his laugh.

Evie straightened. Started to place the dryer on the sink counter, then turned it on him at the last second. "Are you really you, or are you Alex playing a trick on me?"

"I'm me... Right?" Scratching his chin, he frowned. He felt like him. What the hell?

"Alex can appear as anyone she wishes. She's been practicing that fun game on me."

Surprise lifted his brows. "So she *is* a caster?" The last time he saw Alex, she didn't have the aura Evie did, so he couldn't have said if she was or wasn't. Could powers come in so quickly?

"That's fantastic," he said, genuinely happy for her. The fear Evie had she was an anomaly within her own family was no longer an issue. Sharing it with a least one sister must have meant the world to her.

"Yeah." She unplugged the dryer before shoving it into a drawer. "Annoying, too. She turned into Chester the other day. I thought I was cussing out the damned cat until her voice came out of his mouth with the threat to clean his litter box with my toothbrush. Ever since Chester showed up, she threatens me with his litter all the time. I think she's obsessed with that irritating creature."

He laughed. Catching her sliced gaze, he cleared his throat. "Sorry, babe. That must have been shocking to hear the cat talk." He even said it with a straight face.

"Eh, not as shocking as you might think," she mumbled out the side of her mouth. She grabbed a rubber band thingy, then pulled her hair into a springy, coiled pile on top of her head. "But Alex isn't the only one getting a grip on her power. I told the voices to stop today—and they *listened*. I'm finally taking control. I might even *like* this crazy power. Isn't that amazing?"

"You've always been amazing. The power makes no difference."

Taking in the messy hair, flushed cheeks, and bare legs, Shane decided he'd never seen a woman so completely and effortlessly sexy. She was the perfect blend of casual and proper, of delicate and strong. There wasn't a day he didn't discover something new and amazing about this woman.

"God, you're beautiful," drifted off his lips with a shaky exhale.

Her smile was calculating as she sashayed across the floor. His gut clenched at the sensual sway of her hips. She wrapped her arms around his neck, pressing her curves into him. Her lips brushed over his. "Did you miss me?"

"I always miss you," he admitted in a husky voice. His fists knotted her tee, using it to draw her closer.

"I missed you, too," she breathed against his mouth, and then she was kissing him. Gently. Teasingly. Her hands slid under his shirt, and she glided her fingertips over his sensitive skin.

It took all his effort not to sling her over his shoulder, toss her on the bed, and feast. Despite his very pressing interest in doing so, it was not what she needed. The wreck had left her battered and bruised. Less than twenty-four hours ago, he'd feared she might have a concussion.

Regretfully, he drew back. "As much as I would love to take this farther, you're in no shape for what I have in mind."

She groaned. Then her chest heaved with a sigh. "Sadly, you're right. I'm exhausted. My body hurts, and I've been fighting off a migraine all day."

Guiding her into the other room, he said, "Get in bed. I'll massage your cares away, and then we can get takeout for dinner. What do your sisters eat?"

"We love Chinese." She turned to peer at him. "You don't have to baby me, you know. I like it—a lot," she added with a smile. "But it's not necessary."

"It's not babying. After everything you've been through, I want to make things easier." He brushed his thumb along her bottom lip. "What sort of man would I be if I didn't do everything in my power to care for the woman I love?"

"You do love me. Don't you?" Her pause was weighted. "Does it bother you I haven't said the same?"

Cockiness curved his lips. "You have, just not in words."

"Oh, have I?" Her scrunched expression conveyed skepticism.

"Sure have," he said, hooking his thumbs in his pockets and rocking back on his heels "Your aura softens into a mushy, fluttery mess of pinks and yellows."

A scoffing laugh burst from her lips. She made a show of mulling it over. The dark pile of curls bounced when she shook her head. "Nah… I don't recall any mushy or fluttery."

"No?" Shane gripped her hips and reeled her in. Tipping her chin up, he held her gaze as he lowered his mouth to hers, stopping just short of touching. Varying shades of pink infused her aura, gradually fading to yellow the farther away from her body. And there was definitely mushing and fluttering going on. He drew back with a triumphant smirk. "I call your bluff."

Her mouth twisted in effort not to return his smile. "You're feeling pretty proud of yourself, aren't you?"

"I am."

"So, know-it-all, if you know how I feel, there's no need for three little words."

Clever little witch, wasn't she? "Never is a long time," he said, pretending to consider it. "But if it takes twenty years, that's fine. I'll still be right here."

"You're ridiculous." She laced their fingers together. Her eyes held his. "And twenty years is too long. I should have admitted my feelings a long time ago. As a woman, as a witch, you are my everything. I do love you, Shane."

"I know." Shane gripped her face, drawing her closer. This time when they kissed, there were things between them, spoken and unspoken, which bound them. Though he'd sensed her love, to hear the words from her lips made his heart soar, and he knew, without a doubt, there was nothing they couldn't face. Together.

After her night with Shane, Evangeline felt better than ever. They were solid. She was finally getting a handle on her power. And her shift was not only quick, but painless.

When Evangeline had learned her boss' boss would be in town, prior experience had taught her to dread it. But this visit was going better than expected.

Mimi was so preoccupied with impressing Celia she forgot about Evangeline. Left alone to do her job, she accomplished more in those few hours than she had since starting at the library.

Returned items were shelved. New books were put on the carousel display. Books on lend from other libraries were logged in and arranged in alphabetical order by requesting customer's last name.

It was amazing how quickly she checked off each task when Mimi wasn't hovering, commentating, or breathing down her neck. She finished all the items on her to-do list, then moved on to cleaning. By the time her shift was ending, she'd wiped down every surface known to librarians, rinsed out the coffee/tea pot, and organized the office.

She glanced at the clock. Less than half an hour to go with nothing to do. Releasing a drained exhale, she sank into the cracked plastic chair at the break table and stretched her legs out in front of her. Now that she was still, her exhaustion threatened to drag her into its cozy, dark abyss.

She would let it, too, just as soon as she got home. Well, maybe a steaming hot bubble bath and *then* sinking into blissful oblivion. Yes, that sounded like heaven, especially since an unconscious mind couldn't dwell on silly things like powers, jealous ex-girlfriends, and whoever might be trying to off her.

She wanted to believe the wreck had been an accident, but every time she replayed the events, she knew it wasn't. Ramming someone in the ass sent a pretty clear message of intent.

But why? What could she have possibly done to make someone so angry?

A vision of Freya, shaking with rage, flashed through her mind. Yeah, that one definitely hated her, had from the moment they'd met. But did she boast the mental issues to cause a wreck?

"Oh, yeah, that cow is mad enough," Evangeline declared.

"What cow?"

Her eyes popped open to find the new girl—Brandy? Sandy? No, Candy. Hell, was it Mandy? Evangeline couldn't remember. "Hey...Andy." Evangeline was almost certain her name wasn't Andy, but mumbled fast enough, who would notice?

Sliding her bum to the back of the chair, Evangeline said, "Just my nemesis."

A muted ringing sounded. Evangeline craned her neck around until she realized it was her cell, ringing from inside the file cabinet. She yanked open the drawer, dug through her bag, and freed the phone with an, "Aha."

Mallory flashed across the screen.

Evangeline frowned. Her gaze returned to the clock, confirming it was still a little before three. Why would Mallory be calling her when she was supposed to be in class?

Shaking her head, she pressed the *accept* button, lifting the phone to her ear.

"Hello?"

"Evie...get me," came through on a string of static.

"Mal, what?" She hunkered in her chair and plugged the opposite ear with her finger, as if that would somehow secure the connection. "What did you say?"

"I need... get me... in trouble."

"You want me to get you in trouble?" she repeated, which couldn't be right. Annoyance gurgling up, she said, "Say it again."

"I'm in .... Principal ...to suspend me." Mal's frustration came through loud and clear. *"Come get me!"*

Evangeline jerked the phone away from her ear at her sister's shout. That came through no problem. Gingerly returning it, she said, "I'm coming to get you. Be there in a bit."

"Everything okay?" Andy-girl asked with a look of concern.

"Not usually." Shoving her phone into her purse, Evangeline yanked the bag from the cabinet and went in search of Mimi. Just when her day was going so well, too.

Worry pooled in her gut. What in the hell had happened with Mal?

Chapter Eleven

Shane parked in front of Evangeline's. He climbed from the cab and stared at the giant house, debating how to convince Evangeline that she was in real danger.

He hadn't broached the subject last night with Evie, but his mind had been spinning with it. The rumors no one in their right mind would believe were true—his ex-girlfriend was a witch. He recalled a time when they were dating that someone called her as such. He'd thought it was a euphemism for bitch, because she certainly could be. Freya had laughed it off, joking about how her ancestors on her mother's side were rumored to be powerful witches, and wouldn't that be cool? Surely he didn't believe she was actually a witch, right? He had joined her little chuckle fest, assuring her that no, of course he didn't believe it. Who would?

He sure as shit grease believed it now.

Despite seeing it with his own eyes, he still had trouble reconciling it. A caster's power was fueled by their emotions. Freya had none. At least, none he'd witnessed.

Yet, the burst of chaotic energy hadn't been his imagination. One minute, she was her normal, frigid self. The next, she was surrounded in swirling streams of murky red and orange. He shuddered at the rage that had passed over her face when she'd watched Evangeline speed away.

The gate parted at his approach. He grinned. Not a Winther or a witch, but the house liked him. Just as he was about to pass through, a red Honda came to a colon-clenching halt behind his truck. Teetering sideways, he scowled at the inch and a half of space between their bumpers.

Carrow bolted out, slamming the door. She frowned at him. "What are you doing here?"

"What are *you* doing here?" *And how the hell do you have a license?*

"I was invited." Her scowl deepened. "You're not needed for this."

Offense rang through his bones. Straightening his spine, he returned the look. "What the hell does that mean?

Needed for what?"

"The protection spell," she said. Then considered him. "You're not here for that."

"No." A chilly wind swept along the nape of his neck. Hunching, he shoved his hands into his pockets and headed for the porch. Turning to see she'd followed, he asked, "Protection spell?"

Carrow sucked her teeth. Her eyes narrowed shrewdly. "I don't know if I should tell you."

"Why not?" he demanded, lifting his fist to knock. The door responded as the gate had, swinging inward on its own.

"Huh. The house likes you."

"Seems so." Shane entered, stepped aside so she could do the same, then shut the door behind her. "It's a little nuts."

"It's a big deal," Carrow muttered, her gaze skimming over the foyer. "It wouldn't open to just anyone. It's very protective of its Winthers."

Crossing his arms, he said, "Speaking of protective, why are you casting a spell on the house?"

"It's not for the house, fool. It's for you."

"Me?" He blinked. "I don't need protection."

Carrow shrugged. "Our girl thinks otherwise."

He ran a hand through his hair. *Our girl* didn't sit well with him. It implied a comradery he wasn't feeling. "Well, *my* girl was the one run off the damn road."

"Run off the road?" Carrow asked, and a bright streak of yellow wound around her. "When?"

He couldn't help cocking his brow in an *Oh, you didn't know?* "Last night."

"What?" Her features drew together in a pensive frown. "She never mentioned it to me this morning. Is she all right?"

"She's fine," he admitted grudgingly. "Just banged up and shaken. Her car is done, though."

"That thing was done before the wreck," she answered with a snort. Swiping her palms down her face, she asked, "Who ran her off the road?"

Shane folded his arms. Even though the colors swirling through her aura implied concern, he poked anyway. It was the least a good boyfriend would do. "I was hoping you could tell me."

Surprise swiftly changed her energy from yellow to white. He figured the spikey edges that appeared a moment later meant he'd insulted her. Good.

She planted her hands on her hips. "Why would you

think I could tell you?"

He shrugged, letting her stew as he watched the swirl of colors. He was new to this guardian gig, so his impressions could have been as far from reality as the moon, but she came across as nothing but concerned for Evangeline.

"I don't trust the people you introduced Evie to."

She jolted as if he'd slapped her. "What? *Why?*"

"At least one of them wishes her harm. And I really don't like the snake."

She sputtered a laugh. Baring her teeth, she gritted out, "You're high. We finally have the chance to be a full coven again, with a *Winther* at the helm. No one is going to risk that." Her finger came up to poke him in the chest. "Besides, I can read power, better than you ever will, newbie, so I would know if one of ours wanted to hurt her."

Shane rocked back on his heels. She'd definitely taken that personally. Sincerity rang through her aura, so he didn't doubt she meant every word. But believing it true didn't make it so. His gut was knotted with the certainty that someone inside the coven wasn't who they pretended to be. Shane trusted his gut over Carrow's misplaced loyalty.

Curling his fingers around her pointer, he moved it

aside. "Don't ever put your finger in my face again. I may not have the power to hex you, but I'll break the damn thing off."

Her eyes narrowed. For a breath of a second, he wondered if she'd put a hex on *his* ass. He would be righteously pissed if she turned him into a toad. "You're not going to turn me into a warthog, are you?"

He was man enough to admit his sphincter relaxed when she snickered. "Fair enough. I won't finger point or turn you into anything. But don't accuse me of hurting Evangeline. I would never."

"I believe that." He studied her, debating whether to bring up her previous statement. Deciding it was better to know than to wonder, he said, "You said you could read power—I thought only guardians could do that."

"Normally, yes, that's true. But there are a few, and I mean *few,* casters who see power. And even fewer of us can read what kind."

"And you're one of those?" he guessed.

She nodded.

"Can you see I'm a guardian?" he asked. "Do I have... colors?"

"No. Guardians do not have power. You are able to see our auras because we have a crap ton more energy than a normie. But it's the aura you see, not the power."

Huh. That was a very straightforward way of confusing him. "But if I see the aura, then it's definitely a witch I'm looking at. Right?"

"Yes, that's a safe bet."

He knew it. At least he'd guessed something right. Elation bubbled in his chest. "Tell me about Freya Stone."

"Do what?" Carrow gave him a half frown, half smile that could only be described as bland curiosity. "She's a cold, snobby, spoiled brat. Which I'd think you would know better than me. Why?"

Shane knew more than the all-powerful Carrow. *Ha!* Was it wrong to gloat? He didn't think so. Smiling, he answered, "Freya is a caster."

"Bullshit." Carrow laughed. The smile faded the longer she waited on the punchline. The joke was on her. He'd read Freya like a book that Carrow, apparently, couldn't even open.

"Saw it with my own guardian eyes."

Amusement gone, Carrow shook her head. "Freya is no caster."

"Or…" Shane clicked his tongue against his teeth. "Maybe you're not the great and powerful Oz you thought you were." Oooh, that was gonna chap some ass.

The already-lanky woman stretched herself to full height. Despite her promise not to brandish her pointer, she unholstered that finger like a gunslinger straight from the Wild West. "You listen—"

Whatever threat she had locked and loaded was cut off by the squeal of tires skidding across asphalt.

Evangeline cranked the wheel on the Mustang, an attempt to maneuver it into a parking space. With no power steering, she could have parked a tank better. She had to back up and realign three times before she finally straightened the damn thing between two lines.

"You may be beautiful, Rosita, but you are an asshole to drive." Pocketing the keys, she shoved her purse under her arm and struggled from the car. It was so low to the ground she would have had an easier time rolling out the bucket seats than forcing her legs to stand.

"Asshole," she grumbled, shutting the door with a bit more force than necessary.

Studying the brick high school, Evangeline wondered what happened to make Mallory call her. Especially in the middle of her school day. From the moment she was born, Mal had been low-key and independent, preferring to handle life at her own pace and terms. If any of them were capable of facing a crisis without losing their shit, it was Mal, but even shrouded in static, her panic had blasted through the phone line.

Evangeline ducked her head against the chilly wind as she started toward the wide double doors. She made it halfway before Mallory burst through them.

Evangeline stopped, but Mal kept going, bustling past her without a backward glance. "Mal, what—"

"Let's go," she hollered over her shoulder.

Evangeline watched her sister slow at the Mustang before opening the passenger door and tossing her book bag in. She gazed back at her with impatience. "Why are you driving this?"

Evangeline returned to the car at much slower clip. "First, I'll ask the questions. Two, I wrecked mine last night."

Without waiting for a reply, Evangeline slid into the bucket seat from hell and buckled in. Mal followed suit, settling in to stare straight through the windshield.

Evangeline openly studied her. She sat rigidly, her hands clasped together in a white-knuckled grip. If not for her silence, Evangeline might not have noticed her chin quivering with the effort not to cry.

She couldn't remember a single instance—in her entire

life— of Mallory not stating the cold, hard truth of a matter, but her vulnerable demeanor prompted Evangeline to reach for that blazing knot of power in her chest.

Oh, how the tables have turned, Evangeline thought.

Once terrified of the whispers, she now called them up like she was ordering takeout. "Do you want to tell me what happened?" she asked in a soft, neutral tone. She didn't want to come across as accusatory, not when Mal was on the verge of breaking down already.

"No."

I don't know what happened.

Evangeline blew out a long breath, using the pause to gather her thoughts. She reached for Mal's clenched hands.

Mal threw herself against the passenger door, raising her hands out of reach. "Do not touch me, Evie. I swear to God, don't touch me."

The vehemence in her voice shocked Evangeline. She not only dropped her hand, but also pressed against her door as well. "Jesus, Mal, what the hell happened to you?"

Her shiny dark hair undulated like a curtain as she shook her head. She let out a shaky sigh. "I don't know. Just take me home. Please."

Though Evangeline listened with her gift, she heard no underlying whisper. Mal wasn't lying, but the truth didn't reveal anything of what happened either. Had she gotten into a fight? Mal usually kept her cool, but it wasn't unheard of for her to lose it and knock someone upside their head. Or punch them in the gut. Or plant her foot in their dangling genitals.

"Don't I have to speak with your principal?" she asked.

Mal shrugged. "He has his hands full right now. Asked that you call him later."

Again, no whispers. What could he possibly be doing that took precedence over what caused her sister to leave early? Evangeline considered marching inside and demanding a meeting. It wasn't as if she was getting anything out of Mal. But her sister's behavior brought out her protective instincts, and she decided to get her home where they could talk about it in private.

"Sure," she said, cranking Rosita to life. "But this isn't a finished discussion."

Mal rested her head against the passenger window.

Not encouraging.

Evangeline backed out better than she'd parked, but it still took two attempts to avoid scraping off layers of Rosita's red paint. Two days of driving the vintage car convinced Evangeline she never wanted to do it again.

Power steering, satellite radio, and gas economy topped her must-haves for a new car.

Evangeline stopped at the sign as a police cruiser pulled into the school parking lot. The officer scanned Rosita with appreciation before nodding grimly to her. She glanced at her sister. "Mal, a cop just arrived. What happened?"

I don't know.

Evangeline scoffed. How could she not know? Mal was clearly involved somehow. Cops didn't randomly show up to high schools unless called, right? "Well, why were the police called?" And why was Mallory allowed to leave if the issue was enough to call 911?

Questions swirled. Mal wasn't answering. Not even when Evangeline focused on her power, listening with every cell in her body.

Not wanting to draw the officer's attention more than the car already had, she pulled out and headed home. She tried to figure how to draw Mallory out, at least enough to know what happened, if not her involvement.

They were only two or three blocks from home when the whispering started. Only it wasn't whispering. They shouted in her head so loud and all at once that she couldn't pick out a single voice, much less understand what any of them were saying.

"Oh my God," flew from her lips. She clamped her palms against her ears. But the shouts ricocheted around her skull, undeterred by her attempt to mute the volume and maintain her sanity.

"Evie, what the hell?" Mal's squeal cut through the noise.

Evangeline shook her head, squeezing her eyes tight. "They won't stop!"

"Pull over," Mal yelled, and Evie realized she'd not only let go of the wheel, but was also driving blind.

Her lids flew open. In her panic, she'd stomped on the gas. They weaved wildly back and forth across the pavement. Mal was grappling for the wheel as it spun one way, then the other, not quite able to get a grip on it.

Evangeline slammed her foot on the brake. If Alex heard of how she was driving her precious Rosita, she'd never hear the end of it.

Nothing happened. She pressed again, practically standing on the pedal.

Danger!

An insane laugh burst free. "No shit," she howled, stomping for all she was worth.

Though they'd lost some speed without her foot on the

gas, the brakes weren't doing shit. The house was just ahead, the voices were singing *Hallelujah*, and Mal chose that moment to add her screams to the melee.

"Stop the car," she shouted.

Evangeline chanced a quick peek at her. Mal was sitting straight up in her seat, hands braced against the dash as she stared through the windshield in horror.

"I'm trying," Evangeline shouted over the voices. Just because they weren't filling Mal's head didn't mean Evangeline didn't need to yell. "The brakes aren't working."

She watched numbly as Mal threw the gearshift into neutral, then grabbed the long lever between the seats and yanked. It made a mechanical clicking noise as the parking brake engaged.

The wheel jerked a hard right, and the car jostled over the curb. Evangeline didn't have time to correct back to the road before they came to a sudden, jarring stop.

Dazed, Evangeline sat statue still for a heartbeat. Or ten. It was hard to count when her pulse was racing out of control. Smoke billowed up from the front of the car, bringing her pounding heart to a standstill.

Releasing her seat belt, she leaned forward to stare over the hood.

She swallowed the lump in her throat. It wasn't hopping

the curb that had stopped the car.

It was the big oak tree in the front yard.

Mal stretched her spine for a gander as well. Then slowly turned to her. "You're so dead."

Evangeline sighed. "Yeah."

Because Alex was going to murder her.

Chapter Twelve

Evangeline was contemplating running away from home when the door was yanked open. Shane crouched next to her, his dark gaze rolling over her and Mallory. "You two okay?"

Jesus, Evie. What the hell? whispered through her mind.

"I couldn't stop. I pressed the brakes, but nothing happened. If Mal hadn't pulled the emergency brake…" She shrugged, at a loss for words. Tears stung behind her eyelids. Her chin quivered with the effort to keep them from spilling.

Shane tipped her chin up so she'd look at him. "It's okay. Why don't you go inside? I'm going to look Rosita over, make sure she's… fine." He nodded slowly, holding her gaze until her head undulated in agreement.

She didn't remember stepping out of the car, but she was suddenly halfway to the porch. Glancing over her shoulder, she saw Mal moving under the same stiff-legged zombie walk.

The door swinging inward barely registered. Evangeline ambled into the foyer. Calm wrapped her in its warm embrace. She paused, closed her eyes, and exhaled a long stream of air. It wasn't enough to right her world, but it was a start.

"What live wire have you been sucking on?"

Evangeline pried one eye open. Carrow was standing before her, hands at her waist, gaze bouncing from her to Mal. Her glare snagged on Mal, grew comically wide, then swung back to her. "Holy shit," she hissed, side-stepping Mal to inch closer to Evangeline. Her friend wouldn't even peek at her sister.

Mallory shot Evangeline a questioning look. Had Carrow sensed power in Mal? Though her curiosity was piqued, Evangeline shrugged. There were far more pressing matters at the moment.

One of which came pounding down the stairs, giving Evangeline an instant eye twitch. Mal gave her a sympathetic wince. Ellery was still in school for another fifteen minutes. That left one sister in the house and unaccounted for.

"What was that? I heard a crash." Alex paused to scan the three of them. Her gaze caught on Carrow, then darted to Mal. "Why are you home early?"

"My, my, you ladies are fascinating," Carrow muttered under her breath as her gaze scanned each in turn.

"It's only half an hour, not that early." Mal turned her head to face Evangeline. "Nice knowing you."

"Shut up," Evangeline hissed under her breath. Forcing a smile, she addressed Alex. "Just a door bang. You should go back upstairs."

Alex wasn't buying. Her eyes narrowed to slits. "The door doesn't bang here."

Shane chose that second to prove her wrong as he burst into the foyer. The door banged into the wall behind him, and Evangeline shot her sister a *told you* glare. But then her love, bless his sweet, helpful heart, sealed her fate with four little words.

"The brakes were cut."

Evangeline actually felt her lungs shrivel. Yay, wrecking Rosita was not her fault. Boo, because she was going to die ugly anyway. Rosita may have been forged from metal, but she was Alex's baby. Alex took care of her better than any mother took care of their kid. And she'd trusted Evangeline to do the same.

Alex, cluing into what brakes he had been referring to,

and thus to which car, put two and two together and came up pissed. Her face crumpled as she practically flew over to look out the front window.

"Oh, *fuck* no!"

Squeezing her eyes shut, Evangeline braced for a full-body assault. At the very least, a broken nose, maybe a few ribs. Definitely some hair loss. But instead of pile-driving her, Alex raced from the house on a stream of obscenities.

"That went better than expected," Evangeline mumbled with amazement, watching her sister hop around the car.

"How many sisters?" Carrow asked, drawing her attention from the scene Alex was causing at the curb. Carrow studied Alex with fascination. Evangeline couldn't blame her—an Alex temper tantrum was a hell of a show.

It was a good thing they didn't have close neighbors. Even so, one of the businesses down the street might call the cops with all the F-bombs and threats flying from Alex's lips. She acted like a rabid dog with Tourette's. And the ability to set shit on fire.

"Three." Shoulders drooping with resignation, Evangeline added, "I should probably go out there and let her kill me."

"You need to stay in the house." It wasn't a suggestion. When Evangeline raised a brow at his tone, Shane lifted his shoulders in challenge. "I meant it. The brakes didn't fail, babe. They were *cut.*"

"Also, I've never seen spikes that high. I wouldn't go anywhere near what she's putting out right now," Carrow stated.

Resting her hands at her waist, Carrow snickered as Alex kicked the tree, telling it to, "Eat dirt and die, trash."

Because the tree was clearly at fault. Evangeline shook her head.

"Alex isn't the threat I'm worried about," Shane tossed out with more bite than the situation called for. His pointed glower was aimed at her friend, but damned if Evangeline knew why. Come to think of it, they'd both already been here when she got home. What happened between them?

"That's because you're not seeing what I'm seeing," Carrow tossed back. "If you *could* see the energy she's throwing off, you'd find a bunker."

"You can see her power?" Evangeline asked, taking in their mutual glowers. Lacing her fingers with Shane's, she gave him a subtle lift of her brows. His response was to squeeze her hand and as he continued to shoot daggers at Carrow.

"Mars can see it," Carrow quipped. Then, nodding behind them, she added, "The other one, too."

Evangeline turned to find Mal poised to sneak up the staircase. Her baby sister froze like a robber caught in a cop's flashlight.

"Oh, no, you're going nowhere." Evangeline marched over to Mal, intending to drag her to the window so they could all witness Alex's meltdown together, like a good little family. After, they'd check her into a psych ward.

Mal spun out of reach with a shouted, "No," before settling next to the fireplace. "I'll stay, but don't touch me."

Evangeline threw her hands up. "*What* is the deal with touching you?"

Alex burst into the foyer. Her scorching gaze lit into Evangeline. "The only reason I don't scalp you right now is because your mechanic says the brakes were cut. Otherwise—" She ran a finger across her throat.

"We're fine. Thank you for asking," Evangeline said.

"My relief knows no bounds," Alex retorted. "In the meantime, we're also without a car. How are you going to get to work—a broom?"

Carrow raised her hand. "We don't ride brooms. Splinters."

Evangeline clamped her mouth shut before the *snaugh* could escape. That visual would stay with her. Alex shot her a murderous glare. She ducked her head, shoving her humor back in a dark corner where it belonged.

"She can drive my truck," Shane offered, a clear attempt to head off another meltdown from her sister. "My shop is close enough to walk, and for anything that requires wheels, I've got a motorcycle."

Evangeline jerked her gaze to his. "You've got a motorcycle?" Wasn't that interesting. And sexy.

"Yeah." He regarded her a moment. A sly grin spread over his lips. "You like that?"

"I think I do."

"Well, hot damn the hot mechanic has a hot bike. Aren't we impressed? Can we please get back to Rosita?" Alex turned her petulant glare on every one of them.

Shane blew out a puff of air. "I can fix her. Body work isn't my usual gig, but I have most the equipment. Mallory pulling the parking brake slowed her down quite a bit. There isn't much damage."

That seemed to mollify Alex. She chewed her lip. "Good. Bill *her*," she said, notching her chin at Evangeline.

"Drama queen," Evangeline muttered with an eye roll. "It wasn't my fault. What part of *cut brakes* don't you get?"

"I get it. I just don't care." Alex crowded into her space until they were only inches apart. "I trusted you with her. The responsibility is yours."

Damn. Put all reasonable like, what was there to argue? Alex was right—when she'd accepted the keys, she'd accepted the responsibility.

Dipping her chin in concession, she agreed. "I'll pay." Internally, she was crying over the hit to her checkbook.

Shane pulled her close. "You know I won't charge you," he whispered into her ear. Over her head, he promised Alex, "Rosita will be good as new."

Evangeline wrapped her arms around his middle and held on tight. What would she do without him? *Probably get run off the road for good*, she thought wryly. Lifting her head, she blinked up at him. "Are you sure you want to give me your keys? I've wrecked two cars in less days." It went unsaid they'd met because she slammed into the back of his truck. Her track record was pretty dismal.

"You didn't run yourself off the road, and I doubt you sabotaged Rosita, so yeah, I'm sure. Besides," he added after stealing a kiss, "I'm counting on Freya leaving my truck alone. You should be safe driving it."

"Oh, here we go. Freya is *not* a witch," Carrow grumbled. Lifting her palm, she added, "Let me rephrase—she is a *total* witch. But not a caster."

Evangeline pulled back to glance between Shane and Carrow. They glared at the each other. "What did I miss?"

"Freya *is* a caster," Shane insisted, his offense clear in his tone. "I saw her light up with my own eyes." The same eyes he was using to scowl at Carrow.

"You disagree?" Evangeline asked Carrow.

"I do. If Freya Stone had a drop of power, I would know. But not once—" she stuck her finger in the air as if nobody in the room knew how to count to one— "not *once* have I seen her spike. There's no way she's one of us."

"Bullshit."

"Up yours, Carlson."

"What's a caster?" This from Mal.

Oh, Lord Jesus. Not the conversation any of the needed right now. Evangeline waved her off with, "Soon, Mal."

But Alex, ever the lover of drama, piped up to fan the flames. "Why not now? She has the right to know what we are. And why you are a target. Are the rest of us in danger?"

Though Evangeline could no longer deny someone did, in fact, want to harm her, she wasn't ready to discuss the matter with everyone in the room. As for the *why* of her predicament, she had no clue. The *who* was the bigger concern, which she needed to figure out pretty damn quick.

"I don't know why someone wants to... hurt me." Evangeline flashed Alex a warning frown. When Alex smirked, she envisioned singeing her eyebrows. With a blow-torch.

"It's Freya," Shane insisted, an edge creeping into his voice.

"Who's Freya?" Alex asked.

"A rich bitch with no power." Carrow curled her lip at Shane. "And *his* ex-girlfriend."

"Oh, a love triangle." Alex joined Mal at the fireplace. She propped one arm on the mantle, offering up a salacious grin. "How intriguing."

Alex didn't seem to notice when Mal inched the opposite direction. What was up with that girl? Keeping Mal in her periphery, Evangeline pointed to Alex. "You're a wanton jezebel."

Alex shrugged. "I know. Jealous?"

Shaking her head, Evangeline backed out of that argument. The last thing she needed was to engage Alex when she was in one of her moods. Instead, she focused on her man. "Shane, why do you think Freya is the one who wants to... hurt me?"

Shane shot a triumphant snort toward Carrow, who seemed most unimpressed. "I was at the bank when you left the coffee shop this morning. Freya followed you out, appearing rather pissy. A murky reddish aura was swirling around her like a tornado. So, I trailed her home. Long story short, there was a black sedan parked in the drive. The front was dented and scraped with baby-blue paint."

Silence followed his declaration.

"Oh." Evangeline knew Freya wasn't her biggest fan, but hated her, wanted to kill her? Rubbing her temples, she suddenly felt ancient. The stress of last few days was catching up with her. She wanted nothing more than a hot bath and a long nap.

"That makes her a bitch, not a witch," Carrow said, starting off another round of bickering between her and Shane. Their shouted accusations ricocheted through her cranium.

Evangeline clamped her hands around her temples, attempting to block them out. Unbelievably, it seemed to make it worse. Their voices grew louder, more high-pitched, until all she wanted to do was take a mallet to their skulls, so they'd understand what they were doing to hers.

"Shut up," rolled off her tongue like a gentle wave.

A shocked hush fell over the room.

The front door clicked and slowly opened.

Elle walked into the foyer, her book bag slung over one shoulder. She paused, freezing when she realized everyone was staring at her. "Uh, what happened to Rosita?"

Annnd there went the quiet. Carrow tossed off another insult for Shane, who called her a jackass. Alex hooted with delight. Lather, rinse, repeat. Only this time with hand gestures.

Evangeline braced against the wall. Her stomach rolled. Bile rose up her throat. She swallowed it down with effort, then gagged. The pressure in her head was nothing next to the mounting tension behind her sternum. It churned and burned up her esophagus until she couldn't hold it any longer.

"*ENOUGH.*"

Holy piss and vinegar. That was not her voice. It *was,* but also wasn't. It was deeper, heavier, and full of grittiness, as if she'd reached into the earth and pulled it free. It left her throat raw, and she could still feel the energy behind her tongue—hot, heavy, and full of power.

She glanced around the room to see everyone staring at her in shock. Carrow, especially.

Her friend's jaw hung ajar under rounded, awe-filled

eyes. Or was that terror? Either way, Carrow was speechless, and *that* was something.

Evangeline nervously licked her lips, straightened her spine, and met each of their stunned gazes. "Stop arguing, or I will make you."

Shit the bed, Evie. You have Voice.

The whisper had come from Carrow. Turning to her, Evangeline stated, "I don't know what voice is, and I don't care. I don't care if Freya is a witch, bitch, or the heifer that's after me. Given our mutual attraction, probably all three. I don't care about Rosita—sorry, Alex—or what new power will crawl out of my ass next."

"That's an alarming visual," Shane muttered behind her.

Normally, his humor delighted her. Right now, she was fresh out of amusement. All of her sisters were together, and whether they realized it or not, they had a serious problem. Carrow had confirmed both Alex and Elle were witches. Evangeline was betting whatever had sent Mallory scurrying from class had something to do with her power presenting itself, too.

Before they could deal with anything outside of the house, they had to come to terms with who—or more accurately, *what*—was inside.

"Elle, go stand by Alex and Mal," she commanded. She

didn't use the power—Voice, apparently—but she left no room for argument. Not that she expected any from Elle.

Ellery dropped her backpack, then took her place next to her sisters. Mallory immediately closed in on herself, wrapping her arms around her middle and squeezing in to make herself as small as possible.

"Ladies, you may or may not have noticed, but we're different here," Evangeline started, wondering how in the world she was going to pull it around to everything that had happened since she'd moved to Whisper Grove.

Alex nodded. Elle looked confused. Mal stared at her feet.

Evangeline really hoped she wasn't making a mistake. Turning to Carrow, she asked, "You're sure about Elle?" Did her baby sister truly see the dead?

Carrow's head bobbed. "Absolutely."

"What about Mallory?" A tinge of guilt rose up at revealing Mallory in front of everyone, but secrets wouldn't save them.

Carrow regarded the sister in question. Her eyes filled with sympathy. "I think she needs to tell you."

Mallory didn't move.

"Mal, what happened at school?" Evangeline pressed, acid bubbling in her gut. Something told her it was going to be bad. That saying *'cut the tension with a knife'* filled her head. Only it would take a chainsaw to break through.

Finally, Mallory lifted her dark head, meeting Evangeline's gaze with dread-filled eyes. "I honestly don't know."

Evangeline listened for the whispers that would indicate she was hiding something. Nothing.

"All right. Give me the sequence of events," she said, mimicking Mallory's stance by lacing her arms around her middle.

Mallory's throat worked a hard swallow. "I went to the nurse because I wasn't feeling well."

"Fever? Stomach ache? Period?" Evangeline prompted, earning a scowl from her sister.

"None of those. I was freezing. Like, colder than I've ever been in my life. It was as if I were standing naked in a blizzard in the middle of class. My fingers were stiff, and my hands turned blue. I couldn't stop shaking."

Evangeline waited. When Mal didn't elaborate, she prompted, "So you went to the nurse. What then?"

Mal's chin quivered. She squeezed her eyes shut.

I didn't mean to. I didn't even know such a thing was possible.

Despair coated the words so thoroughly Evangeline was suddenly overwhelmed with sadness. The weight of it stole a gasp from her.

"She was so warm. I *needed* her heat."

Dear God, what did that mean? What had she done? Whatever it was, Evangeline didn't need to be a witch to see it was tearing Mal up inside. Evangeline moved forward to take her into her arms, to promise everything would be all right.

But Mal bolted for the stairs before she got anywhere near her.

"Mal!"

Instinct had Evangeline dipping into the heat in her chest. She'd hate herself later, but if she didn't get the truth now, she might never get it.

"Tell me what you did."

Mal stopped, one foot on the bottom step. She stood there, shaking, for long minutes. Then her shoulders hunched. Her head drooped forward in resignation. She turned slowly, and it broke Evangeline's heart to see tears glistening on her cheeks.

"I'm sorry, baby girl, but we need to know so we can

help you."

"You can't help me," Mallory whispered in a cracked, watery voice. "I stole something from her I can't give back."

The tension coiling in Evangeline's belly eased. So, Mal stole something. "Okay, not cool, but we'll deal. What did you steal?"

"Her life, Evie." Anguish rippled over Mal. "I stole her *life*."

The resulting silence was deafening. Or maybe Evangeline simply couldn't hear anything over the rushing of her pulse.

Just when she thought things couldn't get any more messed up, the basement door, the one without a key that never, *ever* moved, clicked as the latch disengaged.

The door slowly crept open with a low, halting creak.

"Finally." Chester, who had apparently been curled next to the door, took to his paws and arched his spine in a lazy stretch. His black tail swished back and forth. "I've been waiting for that to open forever.

Made in the USA
Columbia, SC
08 December 2019

84560427R00139